TALES OF OLD GODS AND NEW

KATE MACLEOD

CONTENTS

TAREN AND KEUI

The Taren had left the plains behind shortly after sunrise just as the symphony of birds was dying down and the whispers of things moving through the tall grass was beginning. The only sound since had been its own footfalls, the skittering of gravel it had dislodged bouncing back down the rocky slope, and the rare screech of a hawk circling high above. The sudden cry of a Keui almost at its feet was so startling the Taren's plasimetal body hardened in defensive response, nearly causing it to fall as its long, loose strides tightened.

But it didn't fall, and a momentary thought relaxed its body. It ran silently and leapt to the top of a nearby boulder, scanning the rocky landscape around it.

So many crags and nooks, so many shadowy places. Not like the open grasslands below. The Keui must have thought it could hide here, but there was no hiding from starving Taren, and the three wrestling the lone Keui to the ground were clearly running on the last dregs of jing. They were slow, awkward, their joints stiff and their plasimetal flesh a dark rusty gray, like blood and ash.

The Taren on the rock fingered its energy blades. The fight for life at its feet was none of its business. But the Keui cried out again, one of its attackers prying into its belly aperture with desperate fingers, and the

Taren found itself leaping off the rock, an energy blade spinning in each hand.

Creatures of blood responded to each other's calls, to feed young or protect a pack member or softly nose a sick comrade. The Taren had observed it on many occasions. But its plasimetal stuff came with no such instincts. There was only jing and who possessed it. As the three starving Taren turned to face its blades it saw the Keui beyond, crawling away, its own jing-deprived flesh thick and dark. The Taren alone had jing in abundance, jing enough to outrun them all without even trying. This fight was illogical.

And quickly over; the numbers didn't matter when its jing-rich body moved swift and lithe while the other three were awkward and lethargic. They quickly retreated, not wanting to waste what little they had left in a hopeless battle.

The Taren extinguished its blades and slipped the hilts back into the loops of its belt. It turned to the Keui, which was still backing away.

"Conserve your jing, there is no need to run. I mean you no harm," the Taren said. "Rest, it's nearly nightfall. You'll feel stronger after you generate."

"Thank you," the Keui said, running smoothing hands over its body. Its flesh was dense but not entirely unresponsive; with patience it was removing the marks where the three Taren had grasped its body, where the one had tried to pry its belly open.

"In the morning you should get back to the Keui herds," the Taren said. "There's safety in numbers for your kind."

"I am not like my kind," it said.

"Keui life is hard," the Taren said. "The strong ones leave the others behind, like bait. No, sacrifices. The strong grow stronger and the weak barely make it from day to day. I've... seen it."

"There is no safety for me no matter where I am; I prefer to be here."

"Suit yourself," the Taren said, then leapt back up onto the boulder to look around. It was growing dark fast as the sun sank behind the mountain. Light still reached the grasslands below. A smaller herd of Keui were bedding down for the night near the foothills, oblivious to the Taren creeping towards them through the tall grass. Beyond the grass the shallow sea glistened red and gold in the dying light, and beyond that the sky met the earth. The Taren turned to look up at the mountain, the center of the world, so tall it touched the domed sky at its highest point.

The Keui below was sweeping dust out of a hollow in the rock, preparing to curl up for the night. The Taren hopped down, its feet striking the ground making the Keui flinch. The two spent the night on opposite sides of the fissure between the rocks. The Taren suspected the Keui slept little. When the first light of dawn reached them its plasimetal was as dark and stiff as the night before.

"You're a slow generator," the Taren noted. The Keui looked away, wrapping its arms around its hollow middle, its long braid loops hiding its face. "If those three come back for you they will be really desperate. They might end you. I've seen it more and more, jing-less husks of Keui slowly turning to dust in the grasslands." Still the Keui didn't answer. The Taren looked up the mountainside. "I'm going up the mountain. It will be hard going but I wouldn't object to some company."

"Why?" the Keui asked.

"To look around. I expect you can see the whole world from there. The peak touches the sky."

"Why let me come?" the Keui clarified.

"I mean you no harm, I just find walking alone too quiet." The Taren looked back over its shoulder at the plains below. "I too am not like my kind."

The Keui rose creakily to its feet then gave a nod and the two started the long climb up the mountain.

It was indeed slow-going, the jing-deprived Keui not able to move faster than a shuffling gait. Occasionally the Taren scouted ahead to find an easier route, its lithe body leaping and running over the tops of boulders. It would get to the top faster on its own but it suddenly felt no need to hurry. It was likely a fool's errand anyway. Its last quest to the outer rim of the world had been fruitless: days and days spent walking the circumference only to end up back where it had started, never finding a way out or a clue as to what lay beyond the dome of the sky.

If the mountain had no answer the Taren would need to find other questions.

The Taren guessed they were a third of the way up the mountain when the setting sun forced them to stop. The Keui slumped wordlessly to the ground but the Taren once more found higher ground to scan the surroundings.

The skittering of rock it had been hearing throughout the day might be the work of blood animals, but it suspected the three starving Taren were still trailing them. They were too weak to catch even the slowest members of the grassland herds, this half-dead Keui was the best they could hope for.

The Taren leapt down to the hollow under the rock the Keui had chosen for their camp.

"It's cold," the Keui said. "I feel stiff."

"You will feel better in the morning," the Taren said.

"I don't think I will."

The Taren said nothing.

"How far back can you remember?" the Keui asked.

"I don't know. I never counted the days. I don't think on the past."

"I can remember further back than anyone I've met. I remember long ago things were different. Taren would bring gifts to Keui, and Keui would freely share jing in return."

"I remember," the Taren said, but the memory was an old one, faded.

"One Taren decided that just taking what it wanted was better and then they all were doing it. It wasn't always like it is now."

"I don't think it will change back. It might change, but not back. Something new will happen."

"You hate this as much as I," the Keui said. "You don't feel like a hunter."

"I will not harm you," the Taren said yet again. If the Keui wondered where the Taren had accumulated so much jing without being a ruthless hunter it didn't ask.

"I remember further back than that," it said some time later. "I remember being different. I was a blood animal. I had this form, but blood flesh."

"That's not a memory, that's a dream," the Taren said.

"It's a dream that feels more real than all this."

In the morning the Keui was too stiff to rise.

"Do you not generate at all?" the Taren asked. The Keui tried to look away but its neck wouldn't turn.

"Look, I'm going to share some of my jing with you. I have enough to spare."

It didn't add what a level of trust it was extending, they both knew it.

The Taren knelt before the stiffened Keui, taking one hand in its own and firmly pulling it up to its own belly. The plasimetal flesh was dense and fought the movement but the Taren was stronger.

Then the Taren focused, relaxed, let the aperture in its belly open to expose its glowing core. The Keui's eyes sparkled in the warm light from the Taren's jing. Then the Taren nudged closer and the Keui's frozen hand brushed against the light. It gave a long sigh as the energy flowed into its body, but as soon as its plasimetal was supple enough to move it pulled back, turning away from the tempting glow.

"Is that enough?" the Taren asked.

"It's more than I've had in longer than I can count. I thank you. Please, close up."

The Taren tightened its aperture and rose. It felt weaker, but only barely noticeably so.

The Keui ran its hands over its braids, removing a gold pin shaped like a feather. It held it out to the Taren.

"A gift?" the Taren asked.

"In exchange," the Keui said.

It touched its own hair, worn loose in the Taren way. It separated a thin lock behind one ear and braiding it down half its length, then took the pin and clipped it in place. "Thank you. I am honored to receive the gift of a Keui."

The three Taren closing in on them were not as sneaky as they thought. The Taren turned, energy blades spinning in its hands.

"Back off. You cannot win this fight."

"No, we cannot lose," one said.

"You share jing with the Keui, you share jing with Taren," said another.

"This Keui and I are comrades," the Taren said.

"We can bring you gifts as well. Share a little first to refresh us and we will bring you troves."

"We will be continuing our journey now," the Taren said.

The other Taren made no further argument, just closed in, their energy blades sluggish but still deadly. The Taren spun and fought, easily trading blows with two at once, but while it did the third lunged at the Keui.

The Taren focused on the two in front of it, driving them both back with blows so fast and strong it could feel the jing burning in its plasimetal. Then it turned back to the third Taren.

Which was sprawled out on the ground backing away from the Keui. Or more specifically the Keui's glowing energy blade.

"Run," the Keui said, and the starving Taren did, followed more slowly by its two companions.

"You have an energy blade," the Taren said. The Keui said nothing, just placed the blade against its thigh until it sank into the plasimetal, out of sight.

The Taren slipped the hilts of its blades back into the loops on its belt.

"We know what we are," the Keui said. The Taren nodded agreement.

"You don't generate."

"But you do."

The not-Taren and the not-Keui regarded each other.

"I was the weakest, always used as a sacrifice by the others," the not-Taren said at last. "We were told no Keui could use energy blades, that we couldn't power them. I can't create them, I can't take them into my flesh as you do, but I can power them. The day I found that out I stopped being a Keui."

"I remember further back than anyone," the not-Keui said. "I remember endless days in the company of one Taren. I don't have the word for what we were. More than comrades. More even than two members of a pack of blood animals. We were as one. But it was the first Taren to steal jing. I still remember the screams of that Keui. Those screams rent the world. My life ended that day. I could not be a Taren any longer."

"This world feels false to me, like a game," said the not-Taren. "I found where the sky touches the land and I followed it all around the world. There is no escape that way. I found no answer to the question of why this world is what it is. But I will not rejoin the game."

"You think there will be a way out on top of the mountain?" the not-Keui asked.

"I hope only for an answer. I will see the whole world from there, and it touches the sky."

The Keui who was not a Keui except by choice looked up the mountain and nodded.

The Taren who was not a Taren except by choice started to lead the way but found it was no longer comfortable with the not-Keui behind it.

"I will not harm you," the not-Keui said. "I don't think I could. I certainly couldn't catch you if you were to run. But even so, I *choose* not to harm you. We are comrades. We have trust. I only want jing freely given, as you did this morning. Without that I will choose to starve."

"Comrades," the Taren agreed and they continued their climb.

The top third of the mountain was the steepest, ending in nearly sheer cliffs, but the climb was the easiest the two had faced since they'd left the plains. Gravity was lighter here, or their jing grew stronger, or both. The not-Keui could leap and scramble as gracefully as the not-Taren and its plasimetal was supple and bright, almost the liquid chrome of the jing-rich Keui in the grasslands below who ran too fast to ever be caught and drained by even the cleverest of Taren.

The not-Taren looked back over its shoulder. Their three pursuers were surely left behind now. They didn't have enough left in them to climb high enough to feel these empowering effects.

The sun was low in the west when they reached the summit, or rather a fissure in the rock wall just large enough to squeeze inside. The not-Taren was tempted to keep climbing, the sky was so close it could touch it here at its highest point just as it had touched it low where it met the ground. But something within the fissure was glowing brightly, beckoning, and the not-Keui was already squirming its way in. Its supple plasimetal was giving way, flowing around protuberances. Then it was inside and the not-Taren was once more bathed in that beckoning glow. It followed.

Beyond the fissure was a circular space enclosed by the rocky mountain summit, the sky like a pool of still, opaque water overhead, the last rays of the setting sun barely filtering through, giving a weak, indirect light.

At the center of the enclosure was a pool, and it was this that was providing all the dancing light. The not-Keui was standing over it, its plasimetal form fairly dancing although its body was quite still.

"It's jing," it said.

"Yes, but not just," the not-Taren said. It hovered a hand over the surface but couldn't bring itself to touch it. "Look how it moves, it's plasimetal. Plasimetal completely infused with jing. I feel like it's deep, like it fills the mountain."

"It feels familiar," the not-Keui said. The plasimetal of its face rippled again and again. "I don't remember."

"I think this is where we came from. All of us, Keui and Taren," said the not-Taren.

"It's where our bodies come from," the not-Keui said. "But we are more than our bodies."

The two regarded the pool in silence for a long time. The sun faded away but the sky over the mountaintop had no stars. Everything but the pool and their two shining bodies was lost to the dark.

"Should we tell the others? This much jing free for the taking, this could change things," the not-Keui said. "The world would not be divided into Keui and Taren."

"Think of the climb," the not-Taren said. "Only the strong could make it up here. The ones who truly needed it would be stuck below. They would be left to prey on each other more and more desperately while the strong and the fast grew stronger and faster."

"I fear you are right. And I shiver to think of the day the mountain runs dry." Its plasimetal did indeed give a little frisson.

They fell back into silence but then the not-Taren said, no more than a whisper, "I too have dreamt that I was a blood animal. I feel so alive in those dreams, more even than I do now, and in this moment my jing is singing in my flesh."

The not-Keui said," it was no dream."

"Our bodies came from this pool, but our selves, who we really are, didn't," the not-Taren said.

"I think," the not-Keui said, "I should like to see what is at the bottom of the pool."

"I would too," the not-Taren said, "but not alone."

"I will be with you," the not-Keui said. "We are comrades until the end."

"No," the not-Taren said, "I mean I feel there is a whole other world at the bottom of that pool, and I long to be there, but I can't be the first to see it. I think I mean to be the last."

The not-Keui nodded. "I understand. But I think I'm supposed to be the first."

"We are bonded," the not-Taren agreed and squeezed the not-Keui's hand. "I shall miss you."

"And I you," the not-Keui said. "I have not had a comrade in such a very long time. I shall never forget you, no matter what lies at the bottom of this mystery."

They stayed like that, holding hands, until nearly dawn, then without a word the not-Keui slipped its hand out of the not-Taren's grasp and rolled forward into the pool.

The not-Taren could feel everything the not-Keui felt as it plunged into the mass of plasimetal substance indistinguishable from its/their own molten form. Its/their flesh melted into it. Melted away.

But something fell for three long days, something remained to sink into the source, and something passed through it and was gone.

And then the not-Keui took a breath. It felt something in that instant that the not-Taren could not, and the not-Taren opened its eyes and found itself once more alone.

It dipped a finger into the pool and took in every bit of jing it could, until its flesh glowed too brightly to be looked at directly. Then it turned to go back down the mountain.

The three starving Taren would be the first it touched.

IMPOSTOR APPARITION

The air on the snow-capped mountaintop whirled about itself, stirring up the flakes that dusted the surface of the glacier before rushing down the mountainside, gathering speed but not warmth. It found me in the hollow between the hills out of sight from the temporary village of tents by the river and ran through me like a lance of ice, piercing my gut then melting within me, the cold spreading throughout my body.

The shock of the cold brought me into sudden awareness, but I couldn't make sense of the world around me. I didn't know why I was in the hollow away from the tents, why there was a dead body at my feet. My thoughts kept swimming away from me, hiding behind the beginnings of a headache when I tried to catch them. I didn't recognize the woman sprawled on the stony ground, several pools of blood congealing around her. I felt like I should know her, but I couldn't bring myself to reach out a hand to brush the tangles of hair away from her face.

Something was trying to push to the front of my mind, but it was like a shriek of urgent terror and I kept pushing it back. I was supposed to be doing something, and some part of my mind knew what it was, but if I had to let that horrid screaming fill my mind before I learned just what it was I would rather wait.

Then I heard a man approaching. "Alfreide?" he called, his voice low and only half-awake. The sun had not yet risen and the world was a pattern of grays, but the east was to his back and his outline stood out starkly as he reached the top of the hill. He stumbled down the steep slope, slipping on the frost-coated grass. He had thrown a blanket over his bare shoulders but the knee that hit the ground was bare and he swore briefly, the cold driving him closer to alertness. "Alfreide?" he called again, his tone still inquisitive but edging into real worry with just a hint of self-consciousness at possibly appearing foolish for worrying.

Then he saw the body and all those conflicting shades of emotion clarified into a wail of pure grief. I tried to speak his name but it died on my lips unspoken; I could not remember it. "Sir?" I said instead, then again when he didn't respond. But it was as if I wasn't there at all. Sobs shook his body, and his face contorted in sorrow tore at my heart. I wanted to try to speak again, to touch him, but the control over my own mind slipped and the screaming took over, stoking up the headache but not letting any articulate thought take hold. I cowered at the edge of the hollow, unable to look at the distraught man, waiting for it all to pass.

The man fell silent with such rapidity I feared that what had murdered the woman had come back for him, but when I lifted my gaze from the stony ground and frozen grass I found him with his arms around the still form of the woman but his eyes on a very different woman floating above him.

Or perhaps not so different. They had the same long raven hair, the dead woman's in what had started out as an elaborate weaving of braids now collapsing, the new woman's left loose. The man had pushed the hair back from the dead woman's face and although he had streaked her features with more blood in the process I saw a similarity. The dead woman was a decade or two older, and even in death her face was stern and uncompromising, quite the opposite of the floating woman's beatific openness. If they had been standing next to each other I would have taken them for sisters nearly a generation apart in age, but with one dead and the other floating near the ceiling I guessed I was looking at a ghost and her antecedent.

"Alfreide," the man said, reaching up a hand to touch the glowing face. The ghost smiled back down at him, a melancholy smile, but before his fingers quite reached her there was a clatter of armor and three men came over the top of the hill, one dressed in the armor of a king's guard, the other two in trousers hastily pulled on under night-shirts. Behind them came a woman who was probably of average height but looked tiny in comparison to the towering men.

"Osgar," said the one of the nightshirted men, falling to his knees beside the grieving man and the dead woman. "My God."

"So much blood," the woman said, mindful of the toes of her slippers.

"Who did this?" the kneeling man asked.

"I heard nothing," Osgar said, raising blood-stained hands in despair. "How can that be? I slept only over there." There was a hill between the hollow and the tent, but not a very large one. We were out of sight but the sounds of the camp waking in alarm carried clearly through the cold air.

"The wine, my lord," said the other nightshirted man, not unkindly. "You drank many toasts with the queen's brothers."

"No," Osgar said.

"Osgar has no belly for wine," the kneeling man said.

"Your majesty?" the guardsman asked.

"It's very subtly done," the woman said. "I didn't notice it myself for quite some time, and I notice things."

"She does," the king said, giving her a momentary fond smile. His queen, then, and newlyweds at that to be so pleased at what they knew about each other.

"I don't follow-"

"Alfreide drank the wine," Osgar said.

"All of it?" the guardsman asked, looking down at the body with wonderment.

"She's from the north," the king said.

"He pretends to drink then trades cups with her," the queen said.

"If there had been any sound of a struggle I would have woken," Osgar said.

"And this does not look like it was quietly done," the guardsman said, crouching down to peer at the thickening blood.

"Captain, have the guards surround the camp," the king said. "No one leaves until every tent is searched."

"They may tell any who questions them that they have their orders from me as well," the queen said. "Should it be necessary."

The man nodded and spun on a heel to race up the hill, voice already raised to call to the other guardsmen waiting at the edge of the camp.

"There is no weapon here," the king noted.

"But so much blood," the queen said again.

"I would like to take her body to my tent," the guardsman said as he rose from his crouch. "Perhaps if I clean off some of this blood I can discover the wound. That might give us a clue as to the weapon."

"See to it, Wulfstan," the king said, then rested a hand on Osgar's shoulder. Osgar looked up, his arms tightening around the stiffening body, but then he looked past his king to the woman still floating over him like a canopy. She gave him a gentle nod and he allowed Wulfstan to gather the body up in his arms and carry her away.

"Whatever is this?" the queen asked, and there was a clatter of something made of glass falling against a stone without shattering.

"A box of medicines...?" the king said, squatting beside her to examine what was sprawled half-hidden in the frozen tufts of grass. The floating form kept her gaze locked on Osgar, and he seemed unable to look away from her either. I felt a stab of annoyance. The ghostly form might represent all goodness and light, but what use was it?

I had no eyes to close or lungs to draw a deeper breath, but somehow I stilled my increasingly chaotic emotion-driven thoughts. I still felt odd, swimmy, like I wanted to lie down and let sleep take me, but I forced my mind to focus.

Why was I annoyed? Was something else supposed to be happening in this moment? What was I supposed to be doing? The sense of urgency for I knew not what was driving me mad. I searched my mind again but even though the screaming had gone I had no useful thoughts, no memories, only an ever-growing headache.

"Osgar, do you know what this all is?" the king asked and Osgar finally tore his eyes away from the ghost to see what the queen had found. The queen was holding an empty box, the wood dark with age, the knotted patterns carved on its sides sparking a feeling but not a memory in my scattered mind. It was long familiar, that was all I knew. She moved her hand through the grass, finding glass vial after glass vial, all empty, and setting them back in the box. Then she picked up a bronze bowl no larger than her palm from where it rested on its side against a stone. The bowl was empty, but the inside was streaked with blood. From the way the king kept turning his face away I suspected the smell was intense, musty and coppery as the thick blood dried. The queen seemed less bothered by the gore, more driven by curiosity as she examined vial after vial.

"What foulness is this?" the king demanded.

"I've never seen the like," Osgar said. "What even is it?"

"Blood," the queen said, delicately sniffing at one of the vials. "Look at the labels. Cat, horse, rat, raven. This one says lion, has there ever been a lion in this kingdom? And this one says unicorn."

"Did Alfreide know of this?" The king's anger was rising but Osgar just looked back up at the beatific form smiling down at him.

"You accuse her because she is from the north?" the queen asked. She seemed genuinely curious, but then as a newlywed she would also be new to this court. "But she's lived among you since she was a girl. Your ways are her ways. She told me so herself, just before the wedding. Perhaps Alfreide was murdered because she uncovered it?"

The king looked unconvinced. "But why would a murderer leave it here to be found?"

The queen turned a vial over and over in her fingers. "We should see how Wulfstan progresses," she said at last. "I think it's likely there is no wound. I think all the blood on her came from this bowl. Someone mixed all these bloods together and doused her in it."

"How would that kill her?" Osgar asked.

"Sorcery," the king guessed.

"I'm not sure," the queen admitted. "We shall have to work to discover that."

Osgar looked up at the ghost again and she gave another little nod. I felt another stab of annoyance, again several degrees sharper than her actions merited. What was bothering me about her? Was it her attitude, like the things unfolding beneath her were not rank horror?

The king pulled Osgar to his feet and the queen took his other arm, guiding him over the hill and into the camp. People roused from sleep gathered in whispering groups, looking over their shoulders at the guards standing between them and their tents. The guards stepped aside to let the king and queen with Osgar between them pass, oblivious to both myself and the ghost following. We passed tents in chaos, clothing and objects strewn everywhere, then tents still being tossed by guards who doubtless did not know exactly what they were hunting for.

Then the king pulled back the flap of one of the tents not yet searched and allowed his queen and Osgar to precede him into the brightly lit interior. Wulfstan had laid out the body on a table, a collection of oil lamps and braziers lending as much light as possible to his work. I could not feel it but all of that flame was making the tent uncomfortably hot, judging by Wulfstan's sweaty brow and flushed cheeks. The queen loosened her fur cloak from around her neck.

Wulfstan had worked quickly; the body was already washed and covered in a sheet, the tangled braids left to hang off the end of the table.

"What did you find?" the king asked.

"Nothing," he said. "So much blood but not a mark on her."

"Sorcery, then," the king said, and Wulfstan visibly started.

"The blood, a curse?" the queen pondered. She had brought the box with her and set it on a nearby table. "We found this near the body," she said as Wulfstan examined each vial minutely.

"No, look at her tongue," I said, without a clue why I was so certain, some flash of memory gone before it quite surfaced. Of course no one could hear me.

"I don't really have any knowledge of such things," Wulfstan said.

"There are people I could send for who might," the queen said. The king looked at her with new respect. Definitely newlyweds. Was that why this village of tents had been set up, for a wedding? Murdered at a wedding, why?

"Look at her tongue," I said again, rushing forward, but I had no hands to touch with. This was a startling sensation; I felt like I had hands.

I swear the ghost hanging over Osgar laughed at me. Just a little laugh, but still. The hot prick of irritation at being laughed at disappeared in a flash as I realized if she could laugh at me she could see me.

"You," I said, reaching for her. She recoiled. I couldn't see my own hands but somehow she was aware of them. "Tell them. Look at her tongue. Your tongue, I guess. Tell them."

The ghost blinked at me and I was just wondering how I was going to act that out if she could see me but not hear me when she floated down over her own form, hovering over her like a swimmer underwater admiring her own sun-dappled reflection from the other side. Her fingers caressed her own face, touching the lips, probing at the mouth. It wouldn't part for her, she couldn't really touch the world either, but her actions were enough to get Osgar's attention. He reached out and touched the body's jaw, gripping against the growing stiffness until the mouth fell open. The others in the room watched him in bemused curiosity until something caught Wulfstan's eye.

"Oh well done, my lord," he said, turning the open mouth closer to the brazier to examine the greenish-black tongue.

"What is it?" the king asked.

"No need for sorcery," Wulfstan said. "Not when there's poison. And this is something I have a little knowledge of."

"You can tell what was used?"

"I have a book I can consult," he said, peering deeper into the mouth and gently poking a finger inside to examine the inside of the cheeks.

"Poison," the king said. "If she was given it all there might not be any remaining for us to find to lead us to the poisoner."

"Possibly," Wulfstan said. "If it's rare, perhaps not."

"Poison," Osgar said, anguish twisting his features as he reached for a camp stool, missed, and fell bonelessly to the ground. The ghost floated near him. The hands that danced around him couldn't touch him, but he looked up into her eyes and she smiled down at him and he quieted once more.

My annoyance and irritation with her were growing into a jealous rage. I probed my mind for a why but there was none to be had. I just knew she wasn't supposed to be there, and I reached out my invisible hands to her again, swatting at her outstretched arm. She gave a soundless cry, her mouth a wounded O as the diaphanous white sleeve that was her arm spiraled formlessly for a moment, disrupted by my touch. She pulled herself back together, turning her attention back to Osgar as the sobs threatened to take him once more.

"My lord?" the queen cried in alarm. "Are you well?"

"Oh, I'm well," Osgar said with a bitter laugh. "Too well. Don't you realize what this means?"

The queen exchanged a worried, puzzled look with the king but Wulfstan's sudden intake of breath drew all eyes to him.

"Poison," Wulfstan said. "In the wine."

"Meant for me," Osgar said.

I gasped as my swimming thoughts finally cleared, the fainting ringing in my ears I hadn't even been aware of suddenly falling silent as the memories rushed back in.

All the wine. So much, even for me, even after I had spilled inordinate amounts of it onto the thirsty ground. It had fuzzed my mind, and I had carried that fuzziness with me into the next world. But I was suddenly coldly sober.

Whoever had tried to murder my Osgar, my love, my husband had failed, murdering me instead, but they would surely try again.

My last horrid memory finally came back to me, of waking with a burning in my belly, struggling to rise from the bed without waking Osgar, knowing I was already beyond saving. My only hope had been in that box hidden among my clothing. After so many years of war, of trade routes severed in nearly every direction, my supplies had dwindled, and the damned wine was blurring my vision, making the neat labels illegible in the moonlight in the hollow, far from the bonfires that lit the camp. In the end I had just used everything, relying on the force of my own will to see me through.

My will had never let me down.

I lifted my gaze from my partner of nearly half my lifetime to the thing still hovering over him.

So, if I was me, what the hell was that?

"Your majesty."

The third man from the hollow, a man I now recognized as Hrothgar, the captain of the guard, saluted smartly from the tent entrance.

"What have you found?" King Hereweald asked, for now I knew him too. My son in all but blood.

"Nothing. We have started questioning the guests. Perhaps someone saw something..."

"It was poison," King Hereweald interrupted. "In the wine, meant for Lord Osgar."

"We'll search the wine stores," Hrothgar said.

"It was almost certainly put more directly into his cup than that," Wulfstan, the king's steward, said, "or we'd all be dead."

"What sort of poison are we looking for?" Hrothgar asked.

"An important question," King Hereweald said. "A local poison, or something brought from a distant land? Knowing that could narrow our list of suspects."

"I'll consult my book," Wulfstan said, spinning on his heel to start searching the many chests that cluttered his tent. Wulfstan always did overpack.

"The blood was a spell," I said to the other ghost. "You know that, right? You can tell them? Or just him? I needed to linger here after death, to save him. They will try again. We have to figure out who did this. Do you know anything? What good are you? *What* are you?"

The ghost flinched at the rising anger in my voice but said not a word, just hovered near Osgar, nearly cowering behind him. He looked up at her in concern, raising his arms as if to hold her tight. The king and queen frowned down at him.

"Perhaps you should rest," Hereweald suggested.

"Something is wrong here," Osgar said.

"Well, yes," Hereweald said.

"I'm familiar with all the poisons of this land," I said to the ghost. "I would have detected any of them. This is something else, something new, something foreign. Someone in the queen's party, perhaps one of her brothers."

I fell silent, looking down at my own dead form. The beatific vision all in white was quite alien to me, but so was this gray form. It had been many years since I had given more than a passing glance at my own reflection. I had grown old. The long years of war, of rationing and incessant worry, had left their mark. All of that had finally been over, this last gathering on the banks of the river that was our common border celebrating the joining of our kingdom with that of Queen Aeronwen, the end of war and the beginning of lucrative trade. The king no longer needed Osgar and I, his one-time foster parents and still closest advisers, to give our entire lives over to him.

Just the morning before I had thought, at last. At last I could bring forth a child into peace and prosperity. Too late now.

"Poison," Hereweald was saying. "They say it's a woman's weapon."

"Anyone can use poison and hide behind that axiom," Osgar said. "We should focus instead on motive. The war is over. Who would want me dead now?"

"Someone who wants your voice out of my ear," Hereweald said. "Someone wanting more influence themselves."

"I don't like this line of thought," Aeronwen said. "It makes it far too easy to accuse my brothers and my people without proof. I give my word none of them would do this."

"Nothing will be done without proof," Hereweald promised her. "Wulfstan will discover the poison; we will work from there."

But I saw the look Hereweald shot at Osgar. Her brothers were absolutely the prime suspects. I had to agree. While the toasting the night before had been good-natured on the surface, I had sensed something harsher driving the competitiveness. Had they expected to have more control over their sister than the last round of negotiations had given them?

It didn't quite feel true in my mind. No one could spend more than a moment in the presence of the newlyweds without seeing just how much the king trusted his new wife, confided in her, sought her counsel already. I had rejoiced at it, anxious for Osgar to be just a touch less necessary to Hereweald, a touch more available to me and our soon-to-be family. Why would someone poison him just as he was stepping back? It made so little sense.

"I need some air," Osgar said.

"Of course," Hereweald said.

I was torn. My heart wanted to follow my husband, but I was curious to hear what if anything Wulfstan learned from his books. I lingered near my corpse, watching through the open tent flaps as Osgar hesitated outside the tent. He glanced back at the king and queen, neither noticing him as they spoke quietly with each other. He turned on his heel, heading in a direction I knew would take him to the tent the queen's brothers shared. His ghost followed, as faithful as a dog.

"This was meant to be such a happy day," Hereweald said.

"I know. I feel it too. Everything is rent asunder," Aeronwen said, her hand resting still on my corpse's shoulder. "We shall make it right. Together."

"Is there any in your party with knowledge of poisons? Perhaps they can aid Wulfstan in his search. I know your branch of your family has been traveling for some time. One encounters so many strange new things when one travels, I'm told."

Aeronwen frowned prettily. I had only met her twice before the wedding began, and had one long conversation with her before the ceremony. She had struck me as a good match for Hereweald, intelligent, with a wealth of experience from her childhood spent traveling while her kingdom was occupied by an usurper, and she was very good at reading people. But on occasion the emotions she was projecting had a hint of falsity to them. I had chalked it up to wanting to put a good face on wedding nerves, but I was less sure now. Was she covering for her brothers?

"I can't imagine, but I shall certainly ask," she said at last. She stepped closer to him and he was about to enfold her in his arms when the sound of Hrothgar's jangling armor preceded his arrival and they stepped apart again, pulling themselves into more regal postures.

"We've found nothing, your majesty," Hrothgar said. His eyes were red-rimmed, and I knew not just from lack of sleep. He was grieving for me. A thousand memories washed over me, starting with my arrival at the king's castle at the tender age of fifteen. The castle had seemed impossibly immense, the open moors too wide for one used to the closed-in views of a forest home. Hrothgar had been a new recruit himself then, the few wispy strands at his jawline not even hinting at the full beard to come, and knew the castle no better than I but each time I found myself hopelessly lost it was Hrothgar who stumbled across me, the two of us together finding our way back to more familiar environs. I had known him as long as I had known Osgar, if a shade less well.

"No one saw anything?"

"We are still questioning people, but no. So far nothing."

Hereweald nodded gravely, and Aeronwen rested a hand on his arm.

"Perhaps if I asked personally," Hereweald murmured.

"I don't know-" Hrothgar began.

"I don't know if it will help. But I must feel like I'm doing something. Yes, I'll address everyone and then we'll take it from there. Will you accompany me?" he asked Aeronwen.

"We should appear united in this moment, certainly," she said. "But pray give me a moment before I join you. I worry about Lord Osgar; I want to be sure he eats something and perhaps rests a little."

"Yes, do that," Hereweald said. "A womanly presence might be just what he needs right now. Thank you for thinking of it, my dear."

His queen nodded and smiled, but I felt another stab of hot jealousy. Osgar already had more womanly presence than he needed.

Wulfstan startled me as he came to stand almost within me, leaning closer to get another look at my corpse's discolored mouth.

"Definitely foreign," he said with a frown. At last he had come to the same conclusion I had the night before. He shut the book with a snap then turned to regard his remaining trunks with an even deeper frown.

"It's all right, Wulfstan," I said, although he could not hear me. "If I didn't know what it was, I doubt it is in any of your books. But I thank you for trying."

"Your majesty," he said, turning to the queen. "You said you had people you could ask?"

"Yes," she said, straightening up as if being given a task energized her. "I'll do that now. There isn't a moment to lose."

"No one leaves the camp until we have the culprit," Hereweald said.

"Yes, but I fear until the guilty party is in chains that our dear Osgar is still in danger," she said.

A chill ran through me. He had gone to confront her brothers. If he and I were right about them...

"You're right," Hereweald said. "He shouldn't be alone."

Hrothgar understood the unspoken command and ran from the tent to find Osgar. I followed him out of the tent then rushed past him, a gust of glacier-chilled wind propelling me across the camp. The dull gray tents of Hereweald's people arranged in neat rows gave way to a chaos of brightly colored tents gathered in homey little circles around smaller fires. These tents came from lands far to the south, the sides designed to be tied up to let the breezes through while the peaked top kept off the hot sun. The guards in their searches had left many cords untied and long panels flapped everywhere in the cold wind, slowing down Horthgar but not me.

My panic eased when I reached the brothers' tent and saw two guards standing at the tent opening, watching both the people gathered around the little fire in the center of the tent circle and the interior of the tent.

"Osgar," Hrothgar called out to them as he burst into the clearing.

"He's taken a horse in pursuit," one of the guards reported. "He told us to watch the rest of them."

"The rest of them?"

"One of the brothers has gone," the guard said. "We sent a boy to tell you."

"He didn't find me," Hrothgar said, still winded from his run in armor. "Which brother?"

"Bleddyn," the second guard said.

Bleddyn. I would have been quicker to suspect Andras with his haughty demeanor or Ifan with his quick temper, but Bleddyn had been in a genuinely celebratory mood the night before, even joking with Hereweald's men about who had marriageable daughters so that he might also dwell with his sister in the court of a king that had such a fine selection of wines.

Perhaps lots had been drawn. His fraternal loyalty would dictate his actions.

Or perhaps the brothers weren't even involved. But then why flee? Why just him and not the lot of them?

"Has their tent been searched?"

"Thoroughly," the guards said. "We were searching it when Osgar arrived. But Bleddyn had already gone. If there was something to find, he probably still has it with him."

"You didn't notice he was missing?"

The two guards exchanged a nervous glance. "We didn't think it odd. You saw him last night, sir. We thought it likely he would turn up in someone else's tent."

"But you didn't make sure?"

"No, sir," the first guard admitted. The second just stared off into the distance, his cheeks hot with self-rebuke.

"Osgar will catch him," Hrothgar said with more confidence then I felt. Had Osgar gone off into pursuit in bare feet and a blanket? Had someone at least lent him a blade?

Hrothgar ducked his head to step inside the tent. The two remaining brothers were sitting on camp stools, fully dressed. Someone had brought them a breakfast of boiled eggs and black bread but it sat untouched on the table between them. Ifan sat with his head bowed over hands clasped between his knees but Andras was bouncing one leg impatiently and leapt to his feet when Hrothgar's shadow fell over them.

"What is going on?" he demanded. "We've had nothing but accusations, not a single piece of actual information. What happened?"

Hrothgar regarded him silently for a long moment, but the two of us came to the same conclusion. Andras seemed genuinely in the dark.

"Osgar's wife the lady Alfreide has been murdered," Hrothgar said.

"God's wounds!" Ifan cried. "Why?"

Hrothgar spent another silent moment studying this brother before answering. "We believe Osgar was the target. Poison in his wine. Which apparently he never drank; that was news to me."

"Poison in the wine," Ifan repeated. "We're being made to look guilty. But by whom, and why?"

"We're working on finding out," Hrothgar said. "You see why it's problematic, your brother having disappeared."

"That great fool," Ifan said.

"We did warn him, this was not the place," Andras said mostly to his brother.

"Warn him about what?"

"Apologies on behalf of all of our family and countrymen," Ifan said. "Bleddyn likely was caught in some husband's tent."

"With some husband's wife," Andras added in case it wasn't perfectly clear.

"It's happened before," Ifan said.

"Oh so many times."

"And you know this for a fact?" Hrothgar said. "Which husband, which wife? They must be questioned."

"I don't know," Andras admitted.

"We lost track of him a few wine barrels in," Ifan said. I could believe it. I tried to remember the last time I had seen him, but my memories of everything that had happened after dinner were a jumble of images, and some of them I suspect were more dreams than memories.

"He'll answer for everything once he's brought back," Andras said. "I'll make sure of it."

"Oh," Ifan said. He turned away, suddenly interested in the cold eggs, but Hrothgar had not missed the look of sudden insight that had flashed in his eyes.

"You remember something else?" Hrothgar pressed.

"Only, I'm not sure," he said. "I definitely saw him kissing a woman between two of the tents on your side of the camp. And I saw dark hair, but then it was dark between the tents, wasn't it?" The women of Hereweald's court, like the women in Aeronwen's court, were largely blond to fairish brown. Only one of us had truly dark hair.

Hrothgar took a deep breath. "Are you saying you saw your brother with Alfreide?"

"Maybe."

"She's the only woman in camp with dark hair," he said. "She's the only one here from the northern tribes."

"Yes, but it was dark. The night, I mean. Between the tents."

"Hrothgar," Andras said suddenly. "You must send men after my brother and Osgar, at once."

"You think he knew your brother was making advanced on his wife?"

His very drunk wife. I couldn't even pull enough memories together to work out whether it was true or not. I had memories of Bleddyn, but always at the bonfire, my husband at my side. Osgar never left my side, not when I was working to keep him sober. He never let me stray from his sight. It couldn't have happened.

Oh how I wished I could be more sure.

"You think that's more worrisome than the fact that he surely believes my brother murdered his wife?"

"He's not a man to act rashly," Hrothgar said.

"With respect," Andras said, "I doubt he's ever been tested like this."

Hrothgar considered, then gave a sharp nod. He exited the tent then strode to the edge of the camp where the horses were sheltering in another hollow. He was giving instructions to a few of the men he found there, but I continued on past him, letting the icy wind carry me high above the rolling hills. No trees here, never any trees, but for once I was grateful for that. I could see for leagues, nothing but the gray of frost-killed grass, the dark blue of the slow-moving river that meandered through the valley.

To my annoyance I saw her before I saw him. Her white form glowed like a tiny moon lost in the space between the hills. I rushed towards her then saw Osgar pinned beneath his fallen horse. Bleddyn stood nearby wringing his hands.

"I'm sorry, I'm sorry," he was saying over and over. "Your horse stumbled on the loose gravel, but I know that's my fault for making you chase me."

Osgar made a sound somewhere between a grunt and a cry, a plea for the pain and Bleddyn both to stop.

"I shouldn't have done that to your wife. I'm sorry. I was drunk."

"Drunk when you killed her?" Osgar growled from between gritted teeth.

"Killed her? No! What are you talking about?"

Osgar roared, this time as he made a supreme effort to shift the injured horse off his leg, but the animal was too heavy, too unwilling to move.

"She's dead? My God," Bleddyn was still babbling. I was getting the sense that my pounding headache was still hours in his future. He was still deep in the fog of wine.

"Go back to camp," Osgar said, flopping back in exhaustion. "Get help."

"Yes, of course," Bleddyn said, turning to his own horse that was sniffing at a tuft of frost-glazed grass. Then he turned back. "Does everyone think I murdered your wife?"

"Get back to camp," Osgar said again, more firmly. "Quickly."

Bleddyn didn't hesitate twice. He swung astride his horse and rode back the way I had come with all speed.

Osgar let his head fall back against the frozen, stony ground. The ghost had been floating high above him but drew closer now, hovering close to his face and smiling down at him.

"Alfreide," he said. "It's too soon. I can't join you yet. I need to find your murderer. Give me strength. Give me the strength to stay apart from you until this is done."

She continued smiling down at him, lifting her diaphanous arms and setting her loose hair to spinning, as if she were a blanket that could cover him, keep him warm.

"I'll avenge you," he said. His eyes were closed but speaking aloud was keeping him awake. I could well imagine how the cold of the stony earth beneath him was leaching the warmth from his bones, even with the hot weight of the horse above him. "I will find who did this and they shall pay. I swear to you. You will be able to rest in peace then."

If I had been a living being I could have snorted. The vacant bliss on that ghost's face; what more peace was she going to find in rest she didn't have now, floating around uselessly?

Not that I was much more use myself. At least the pretty thing could be seen, could lend some comfort. I settled close to Osgar's side but could not feel the warmth of his body or smell his familiar scent. Sweat and leather and something underneath, just a hint of pine that reminded me of my childhood home, a place he had never been to. How he had acquired that smell, one of the many mysteries of him I had never solved. I focused my whole mind on that smell but it was like reading the words on paper; I could invoke nothing of the actual sensation.

The brothers were innocent, I would swear to it. None of the king's men would want Osgar dead. Was there someone else in the queen's party who stood to gain something by his death? But I hadn't been along for the first few meetings of our two peoples. I barely knew their names let alone their stories.

Aeronwen knew her own people. Could I trust her to question them thoroughly, to discover the name of the poison, perhaps even the poisoner? The night before I would have said yes. The way her eyes, her whole face lit up when Hereweald regarded her, I would swear she would do anything for him. Why today did she feel so false?

I looked up at the beautiful young ghost staying near to my husband, keeping him fighting to stay awake and alive. She irritated me out of all measure. Perhaps there was something wrong with me. The spell so hastily performed, I had not brought myself back as I truly was.

No, I decided on the crest of another wave of annoyance. That ghost was the impostor. Even when I was as young as she appeared I had not been so blithely devoted only to my husband's emotional needs. If she were truly me, she'd be doing something to find the poisoner before he struck again. If she was even aware of the danger she didn't show it, all soft smiles.

The guards Hrothgar had sent arrived at last, Bleddyn leading the way. The three of them lifted the now-still horse long enough for Osgar to pull himself clear. I didn't linger to see them settle him on one of the other horses, or to listen to more of Bleddyn's apologetic babbling. If the brothers were all innocent I had more investigating to do. I soared high into the sky and followed the river until the tent village was once more in view. The sun was climbing towards midday, melting the frost and the ice that had edged the stiller pools of the river, but I still found currents that came from the snow peaks to carry me along. People turned away from my path, drawing hoods and scarves against the suddenly chill wind.

The brightly colored tents of the queen's people were in less disarray than when I had passed through them before. People were repacking the clothing and other belongings the guards had tossed about in their search. Some of the tent sides still hung loose, stirring in the breeze as I moved past them.

But one tent appeared untouched. The queen's tent. Surely it had been searched; it had ceased to be her personal space the night before when she had made the king's tent the first home they would share together. I slipped inside. Her ladies-in-waiting were sitting around a table, needlework near at hand but untouched. They didn't speak, just shared an uneasy silence. The servants were busying themselves sorting through clothing, putting away last night's finery. If the guards had searched this place they had been very delicate about it. Most of the chests stood open as the servants fussed and I could peer inside but I couldn't move even the finest of underthings aside to look deeper, my hand just passed right through.

Then I spotted a small box that seemed to be trying to make itself invisible, tucked under the open lid of one of the chests. I bent down low to get a closer look at the silver clasp on the front of it, the etching of a rose circling around the keyhole. I hovered close to the ladies-in-waiting, searching for signs of a key. None of them were wearing anything on a chain, and nothing was poking out or bulging from inside a pocket.

I went back to the box. It was the closest thing I had to a clue, and it was probably nothing. My headache was returning, despite my lack of head. I focused all my will and reached out to touch that tantalizing lock. The silver tarnished as I passed through it, but before I could even wonder at what this reaction could mean I passed through something inside the box and suddenly I was retching and heaving. I contracted my being and fled the tent, still trying to void a stomach that was no longer there.

I made my way haltingly back to Wulfstan's tent and my corpse, now completely covered by the sheet. It took several long moments for the episode to pass, and even when I could straighten back up and look about without another rush of nausea sending me heaving again I felt... diminished.

I was running out of time.

Wulfstan was still there, sitting on the rug turning the pages of several books at once. If I could bring him to the box he would discover everything. I tried touching his books, but had no effect. I moved my entire body through his and he didn't so much as shiver. I looked around and found a silver spoon on the table beside his neglected breakfast and put my hand over it.

It didn't tarnish. Apparently that reaction was unique to the box. Not that he would have noticed a suddenly tarnished spoon when he was engrossed in his fruitless research.

The guards at the edge of the camp started shouting to one another. Osgar had returned. Injured as he was, he would come here first. Wulfstan didn't look up from his books until two of the guards helped Osgar limp inside. He looked pale and his eyes were wandering, but they came back to his ever-present ghost companion again and again. Wulfstan leapt to his feet and helped guide Osgar to a camp stool.

"You're lucky; nothing's broken," he said after running his hands carefully over Osgar's swollen, almost purple thigh. Osgar barked a humorless laugh and Wulfstan realized what he had said. "Sorry."

"Any progress?" Osgar asked.

"Not as such," Wulfstan said, digging through another chest for a small pouch. He poured some of the contents of the pouch into his hand, dried leaves he crushed between his palms into the cup of ale sitting beside the breakfast he had never touched. "Drink this."

"I don't wish to sleep," Osgar said.

"It's just for the pain," Wulfstan said, but couldn't stop himself from adding, "rest would be the best medicine." Osgar shook his head and tried to rise from the stool but the leg wouldn't hold him. He flopped back with a curse then swiped the cup from Wulfstan's hands, downing the contents in one long swallow.

"Give it some time to work," Wulfstan said. He looked up but the guards had gone. "I need to speak with Hrothgar."

"Bring him back here; I have words for him as well. And Here-awald." He was too exhausted, in too much pain to correct what sounded like a command to a king.

Wulfstan stopped halfway out of the tent to look back at Osgar. "You'll be all right alone here?" He glanced briefly at my body under the sheet. I wondered if I was beginning to smell yet. The cold was probably preventing that, now that Wulfstan had extinguished most of his lamps and braziers.

"I'll be fine," Osgar said. I doubted he even remembered my body was there, not with the vision of my younger self fussing over him. Wulfstan gave a curt nod and left the tent.

"I wish you could speak to me," Osgar said, trying to reach a hand up to touch the ghost's cheek but she was just out of reach.

"You can speak to him," I said to her. "I need you to get him to follow you when you follow me," I said. "I have something to show him."

The ghost spared me a quick glance, hot anger in her eyes.

"Why won't you?" I demanded. She shot me another look. This time Osgar turned on his stool to follow her gaze and for a moment, one brief happy moment, I thought he saw me there, but then he looked back to the other ghost with a puzzled frown. She smiled down at him reassuringly.

"Wulfstan lied," Osgar grumbled to himself. "That stuff is making me thick-headed." He struggled to his feet, grasping the edge of the table that held my body to help him limp towards the doorway. He grit his teeth against the pain with every step and grew paler than he had been before and the ghost glared at me accusingly, like I had spurred him to action. Did she not know him at all?

"Lord Osgar," Aeronwen said as she appeared between the open tent flaps, a basket filled with bread and cheese hanging from her own arm, her servants left behind. Quite irregular. The ghost recoiled; if she had been a cat she would have been hissing.

"Calm down," I said to her. "No one likes a jealous ghost."

The ghost ignored me, moving to put her form between the queen and Osgar. But the queen moved right through her, disrupting her form into eddies of white light. Osgar blinked but said nothing.

"Please, sit," Aeronwyn said, setting the basket aside to help Osgar back to the stool. "My husband is coming here to talk with you, there is no need for you to stir yourself."

"I don't like waiting for others to do for me," Osgar said but couldn't quite cover the sigh of relief as he settle back down onto the stool, his leg stretched out before him.

"No, of course not," Aeronwyn said, setting the cheese on Wulfstan's table and cutting off a piece with a little silver knife. She smiled at Osgar, a crooked smile, higher on one side than the other, the dimple deeper. I imagined her practicing it for years in any reflective surface she could find. Only long practice would allow something so contrived to appear so guileless. "But you'll indulge me, won't you?" she asked, holding up the cheese. He shrugged and her hand extended, not to give him the cheese but to bring it to his very lips.

The ghost wailed, but if Osgar heard her he made no sign as he chewed the cheese. Aeronwyn broke off a piece of the bread and unleashed that smile again, as if what she was doing was too silly to really be a seduction.

Ooh, she was good. She knew just how much charm to unleash in this moment. She wasn't seriously trying to seduce him, not on this day in this tent with my body cooling at their elbows, but she was definitely taking the first steps down that road. And he was too far from his usual self to realize he was following her.

The ghost tried to put herself between the two of them again. This time Osgar caught the queen's hand and took the bread from her before she quite got it to his mouth and she gave a pretty little laugh but Osgar's eyes were on the ghost, a puzzled furrow in his brow.

"What is it?" he asked. Aeronwyn tilted her head questioningly as she reached for the knife to cut another piece from the cheese.

"What is what?" she asked.

"Something is wrong here," Osgar said, frowning at the wild gesticulations of the ghost.

"Oh," Aeronwyn said, and spared the outline of my body under the sheet a brief glance. "Yes, very wrong. I am sorry that the day after my day of joy will always be a day of sorrow for you. Perhaps someday we can find a way to change that."

Osgar gave her a sharp look and she set the hand she had been offering him cheese with back onto her lap.

"I meant the king and I can help you. I know you and he are close."

"Alfreide and I have been close to Hereweald since his parents died. It has been the three of us working together for this kingdom for more than a decade."

"I'm sorry that had to end so abruptly," Aeronwyn said. "Going forward it will have to be a different three that leads this kingdom. Hereweald and I are going to need you. That is all I meant." She tried the smile again, but there was something else gleaming in her eyes.

A shiver spread throughout my body and I sunk down to the rug amid Wulfstan's books.

I had been wrong. Hereweald had never been in danger. I hadn't died in his place; I had always been the intended target.

I looked up at Aeronwyn once more offering a bite of cheese. She had known, Osgar's and my trick with the wine. She had noticed it, and used it.

Osgar grasped her wrist and pushed her hand away. "Alfreide and I were planning to leave the court. You know this."

"Yes, of course," Aeronwyn said. "I just thought, with her gone, perhaps you would stay among those who love you. You've long been like a father to Hereweald."

"He has outgrown the need for me," Osgar said.

"Oh, I don't think quite yet," Aeronwyn said. "But we don't have to discuss this now," she added with another glance at my body.

"Don't we," Osgar said flatly. She fidgeted under his gaze and broke into a grateful smile as Hrothgar entered the tent followed by Wulfstan and Hereweald. "Ah, my husband arrives at last." She rushed to his side and he gave her a brief kiss before noticing the way Osgar's eyes followed her around the tent.

"Osgar?" he asked.

"Now," I said to the other ghost. "Follow me now, and they will all follow you."

The ghost moved into Osgar's line of sight, her face all heart-breaking sorrow. Then she darted out of the tent, faster even than I although I soon overtook her. Osgar cried out and Hrothgar and Wulf-stan scrambled to aid him as he stumbled out of the tent, following the ghostly form only he could see.

It took a frustrating long time to direct the ghost's attention to the little box hidden under the lid of the open chest, and then for her to get Osgar looking that way, but after some fruitless rooting around in the chest itself he finally slammed the lid shut and everyone's eyes were on the box.

Everyone's but mine. Mine were on Aeronwyn's face. She blanched, but only for half a breath. Then she threw up a mask of concerned puzzlement to cover as her mind furiously worked out what she was going to do next.

Osgar picked up the box and shook it. The tarnish had spread from the lock to engulf the entire box.

"Is there a key?" Wulfstan asked, looking towards the cowering servants then to the ladies-in-waiting standing nearby. Some were shaking their heads but before any could muster a proper response Osgar hurled the box to the ground and it split apart.

"Don't touch it!" Wulfstan said, pulling Osgar back. "If it's what killed Alfreide-"

"It must be," Hereweald said, leaning over the crumbling leaves that lay amidst the pieces of broken box, stirring in the breeze blowing in through the open tent flaps. "But who?"

"Her," Osgar said, his voice dark with anger. The king blinked at him questioningly and Osgar, still leaning heavily on Hrothgar for support, lifted one shaking finger to point to the queen. The ghost loomed over the startled queen, her loose hair and gown spreading wide giving her a silhouette like a bird of prey about to swoop down on the still silent woman.

"Nonsense," Aeronwyn managed at last, drawing herself up straight and crossing her arms to play for time. She still hadn't found the words to turn things back in her favor. Wulfstan snatched her hand, pushing back the heavy weight of her quilted sleeve all the way past her elbow. Something dangled there, tied with a piece of black ribbon close to the crease of her elbow. He yanked it free despite her protest then opened his hand to show the others a little silver key.

No one had any doubts it would fit the lock of the destroyed box. No one even bothered to try. Hereweald started towards her but Osgar stopped him by resting a hand on his forearm.

"Justice," Osgar said. "Not anger, not vengeance."

"She tried to murder you," Hereweald said. His face had gone nearly purple with rage but to his credit his voice was strong but steady.

"I didn't! I never!" Aeronwyn cried, falling to her knees.

"No, she didn't," Osgar said, and the other three men all gaped at him. "It was Alfreide she murdered. Alfreide was always the target after all."

"But...why?" Hereweald demanded. Aeronwyn only looked up at him pleadingly, tears streaking her pale face. Despite her best efforts, it wasn't a particularly pretty sight.

"God knows," Osgar said. "She couldn't allow another woman to have influence over you, particularly not a maternal one."

"Alfreide was like a mother to me," Hereweald agreed. "But so much more than that, to my kingdom. We would not have survived the long sieges without her careful planning."

"I do wonder what your queen's plans for the future were," Osgar said. "What is about to happen that makes it so crucial to remove my wife here and now, on the very first day of her reign as your queen, before we're even back at the castle. Days before Alfreide and I were about to step down..." His voice broke and Hrothgar guided him to one of the padded stools where the ladies-in-waiting had been sitting. Osgar slumped, his injured leg straight out before him. He put a hand over his face as if tired, but all knew he was weeping.

"Take her out of here," Hereweald said to Hrothgar. "She will have to be questioned. I hope this is just her petty jealousy, but if it's a part of something larger..." He sighed deeply. Petty didn't really describe the workings of his queen's mind. Perhaps the dark days were not yet done.

"Yes, your majesty," Hrothgar said, helping the weeping queen back to her feet. All of the women in the tent went with her, clutching each other in twos and threes but none standing too close to the disgraced queen. There would be a lot of interrogations before this camp broke. Probably even more after.

Wulfstan used a tray and knife from the ladies' table to gather up the bits of box and poison.

"This is what killed her," Hereweald said.

"Without doubt," Wulfstan said. "Of course I'll be comparing it to my books all the same. My own curiosity, you know. In case we ever see its like again."

"Of course," Hereweald said. Wulfstan looked like he wanted to grin but a glance at Osgar drained the urge away. Instead he just nodded and carried the tray back to his own tent.

Hereweald put a hand on Osgar's shoulder. Osgar covered it with his own hand, the one not covering his eyes.

"What do you need?" Hereweald asked. He was asking in his most kingly voice. If Osgar asked for the head of the queen, it would be his.

Instead, Osgar said, "I just need a moment. Just a moment, and I will be back at your side and we will sort all this out. Who else knew, how involved were her brothers, all of it. But just a moment first."

"Take two," Hereweald said, giving his shoulder a squeeze then exiting the tent, dropping the tent flaps closed behind him. The ladies-in-waiting had been doing needlework by the easterly light the open tent flaps had given them. In the sudden darkness of the closed tent the other ghost glowed almost too brightly. Osgar blinked as he looked up at her. She smiled back down at him, her hands fluttering around his face as if she longed to touch him. She wasn't the only one.

Her form in my own eyes blurred, the brightness intensifying, like looking into a candle flame after too many hours pouring over maps and lists deep into the night. I had to concentrate to bring the scene back into focus.

I was starting to fade; I could feel it. And yet she was still there, strongly defined as ever. It wasn't fair. I had weakened myself when I encountered the poison, the weapon that had murdered me, but perhaps it was just that the job I had lingered to see done had been accomplished. Osgar was in no immediate danger, never had been. The terms of my spell were complete; it was time for me to go into whatever happened next.

And yet, that other ghost was going to remain.

I longed to be in her place, looking down at Osgar one last time as he looked up at me, as he saw me, really saw me. Why could he see this thing and not me? What even was she? Some side effect of my hasty spell?

Then a horrid feeling shook me. The spell had brought me back, I knew that. But what if I wasn't me? What if she was really Alfreide, and I was just the being created to carry out that last spell? She wasn't the impostor, I was?

How could that annoying thing really be me? Or was it some aspect of the spell that I felt such strong loathing for her?

I rushed up to her, pushing my hands through her back until they emerged from her chest. She writhed, her form struggling to remain cohesive even as I formed fists and pulled my arms back through, scattering her even further. Osgar cried out my name, our name, and the ghost reached out for him as I pulled my fists back to strike again.

But I didn't. The other ghost pulled herself back together and was soon glowing once more, her brightness undiminished.

Maybe I really was me, was the thought that had stopped me from driving here away. I was really me and that ghost some thing that Osgar had summoned with his own mind. Because if a ghost was a memory, it would make more sense for her to be born from his memory than from mine; my memory was decomposing even now within the shell of my body in Wulfstan's tent, but his was still strong.

The thought made me so sad. This was what Osgar thought was me, this young guileless form? But then he had never known me as well as he thought he had, had he? The blood magic was always something I had kept secret from him, even as I used it to keep the remaining cows and goats producing milk despite the meager food we could provide them with during the long sieges. Even as I used it to contain the contagion in the corpses our enemy had used to block off our water supply, hoping to kill us all with plague and save breaking down our walls. He hadn't even known I'd had a grandmother who wasn't from the north but from a land farther even than those Aeronwyn and her brothers had ever traveled to, who had taught me every bit of her craft before sending me off to marry and bring peace with our southern neighbors.

Still, this form of hers felt a bit much. I had seen my body that morning; I didn't look like this young thing anymore. Hadn't he noticed?

A shiver ran through me, something like a laugh. I couldn't be too hard on him; I hadn't exactly noticed the years either. I wondered if our positions had been reversed, as they so easily could have so many times in the past during those endless battles, what ghost would I have conjured of him? And what would he think of the form I chose?

I would like to think I would imagine him just as he was, that I knew him perfectly, but there was no way to test such a thing.

I looked to the ghost still smiling down at him. He wasn't going to need her forever. She would fade in time as I faded from his memory, never entirely gone but eventually not a daily ache. I could take her from him now, but what use was that? I could not stay in her place.

"Take care of him," I said to the ghost. She nodded gravely, rotating around him to take a position just over his shoulder, standing tall and stern with a fierce look to her face that brought her eyes into stronger focus, dark against the pale of her skin. Maybe she wasn't so bad. She wasn't me, she didn't feel like me, but I had other places to be.

I drank in Osgar's face one last time, trying to hold on to every detail, but my thoughts were scattering further and further apart. Then a sudden wind snapped at the loose tent flaps behind me. I thought for a moment that he could see me, that he was looking straight at me, and his lips started to part, perhaps to say my name.

Then the wind changed directions and I went with it, out over the gray waters of the river, roiling in eddies near the ford then narrowing to a channel of fiercer dancing water. The river went on to the sea, but I scattered long before, the last bits of me still remembering the low rumble in Osgar's chest as he used to say my name in his sleep.

Alfreide.

UNSAFE, UNSOUND

E*than*

"There's a dead man coming up the road."

I looked up from my grandfather's old copy of Euclid's *Elements* and blinked away a momentary blindness. It had grown dark while I was reading and Ma had placed a lamp on the table beside me without my even noticing it. Now I couldn't see outside of the small circle of its light. It took a few blinks before I could make out Jacob across the room, ghost-like in his flowing white nightshirt standing at the moon-bright window.

"From town or from out?" Ma asked, setting aside the pair of my father's pants she had been hemming up to my size. After Jacob's growth spurt it was time for me to hand down my own things and make do with my father's, even though they were far too big for me.

"Out," Jacob said. "A long ways, I think."

What did Jacob mean, a dead man? He said such odd things, like the delirium of his recent fever hadn't quite left him more than a week later.

"Get to bed," Ma said to Jacob, taking his place at the window. I got up to peer out over her shoulder. Frost blanketed the dry scrubby grass, glittering in the nearly full moon. The man stood out all the darker in contrast, stumbling in a slow shuffle as he left the road to approach the house.

"What's he want?" I asked in a low whisper.

"Likely doesn't know that your father has passed," she said. "We'll find out soon enough." She wiped one hand and then the other down the front of her skirt; holding that shotgun never failed to make her palms sweat. She had never had to fire it, but the threat of it had come in handy more than once. Jacob lingered in the bedroom doorway, watching with calm detachment. Apparently it took more than a walking dead man to alarm him these days.

The man reached the doorstep and tapped the feeblest of knocks. Ma nodded to me and I opened the door just enough for her to poke out the barrel of the shotgun, aiming it at what should be between the shadow's eyes.

"The doc doesn't live here anymore," she said firmly. "You have to go on up into town."

"Dead man," Jacob said again. "I see him."

"We all see him," I said, although in truth I could see nothing but an outline, a dark patch of space the moon wouldn't touch.

Then the shadow straightened, a hat defined itself and I realized Ma had been aiming at the top of a bowed head, not between the eyes. Eyes that were green on the cusp of brown, just like my Ma's.

"Bessie," he said, then fell to the ground half in and half out of the house.

"Ma?" I asked.

"Help me bring him inside," she said, putting up the shotgun. "Then run and fetch your grandfather."

"But who is he?" I asked.

"Your uncle Si," she said. I had never met him, but knew him well from her stories. She loved telling of all the adventures the two of them had had growing up in this very house together. Jacob and I were five years apart in age and had never been as close as my Ma had been with her brother Si.

Jacob hovered nearby as I helped Ma move Si into her bedroom and onto the bed. He didn't say it again but he didn't need to. I could smell it now, the odor of gangrene.

Dead man indeed.

———

Bess

My brother didn't stir as I pulled crusty, blood-soaked bandages from his wound. I was as gentle as I could be, but the bandages had dried into hard shells hours ago and clung to the wound, refusing to let go even when I soaked them with ladle after ladle of warm water.

He didn't stir: that wasn't a good sign.

Jacob lingered in the doorway, watching me work without saying a word. His face in the moonlight was sharp, all baby fat burned away during the long weeks of his illness. I knew his mind, too, had not yet recovered, although my father-in-law said I was just being silly. I tried to give my boy an encouraging smile, but my mouth wouldn't cooperate. I had longed to see my brother again for so many years, and now that he was back he was going to die in my bed without a word passing between us.

Jacob stepped up to my side, holding a bundle of clean rags. I gave him a nod of thanks. I had cleaned the wound as best as I could, perhaps too aggressively as it was weeping again now. I used the rags to make a new bandage although the smell rising from the wound mocked my efforts. This was only going to end one way.

Someone had dug a bullet out of Si's shoulder and tried to burn the hole clean, the flesh all around burned black, but it hadn't been enough to keep the contagion out. He had walked up to the house alone, I feared he had nursed himself on his own as well, dug at his own flesh with his bush knife, burning the flesh, probably by heating the same blade. Then somehow got to me.

I picked up his belt from where I had tossed it earlier and found the knife, bloody and blackened and scarcely cleaned. I dropped it into the bowl of warm water I had used to wash his wounds, but absent-mindedly as my attention was fixed by the gun holstered on the other side of the belt. I took it out, turning it over and over in my hands. It was scarcely a proper gun, all gleaming silver and mother of pearl, more a piece of deadly jewelry. It was the last thing I'd expect my stoic brother to be carrying about as a weapon. Had the years changed him so much?

Jacob was squatting low, examining the belt buckle without touching it, leaning so close his nose was a hair breadth's away.

"Do you like that buckle, Jacob?" I asked, more to distract him than from real curiosity.

"No," Jacob said firmly and stood up. He cocked his head to one side like a dog listening. "Ethan's back," he said and ran to unlatch the front door. I picked up the belt. The buckle was small but silver and mother of pearl like the gun. There was a pattern worked into it my eyes couldn't pick out in the lamplight, not under the layers of tarnish that marred the silver. Perhaps it was just Jacob's strange reaction, but something about that image I couldn't quite see made my stomach twist. I didn't like it either.

Ethan

Grandfather took one look at my uncle then turned back to me with the scarcest hint of a nod. When I had rousted him out of bed I had told him I reckoned it was already too late. I could see by the tightness of my mother's face she knew it too. She had looked just like that before my father passed.

"I brought morphine," Grandfather said. "Enough to make him comfortable, or-"

"No," my mother said. "He came back to tell me something."

"I wouldn't bet on him being lucid again," Grandfather said. He wasn't being unkind, but then he wasn't trying to gentle his words up any either. I could see them hitting her like blows as she flinched.

"Is there nothing we can try?" I asked desperately. I remembered my mother those first weeks after Dad had passed. I would do anything not to see her like that again.

"Is there?" Grandfather countered.

"Burn the wound?" I offered.

"Been done, tried more than once by the look of it," Grandfather said, lifting up the edge of my mother's neatly tied bandage.

"Amputate," I started to say but then shook my head. "Too far up." The wound was in the shoulder, but closer to his body than his arm. There was no way to cut there.

"He came so far," my mother said. "He has to wake up."

"Maybe he will," Grandfather allowed. "Your people are of a stubborn stock."

"He was hunting death," Jacob said. I hadn't even realized he was there with us in the room.

"How's that?" Grandfather asked, and Jacob pointed to the gun on the floor by the bed. "Well, that's a damn fool errand if ever there was one."

"What do you mean?" I asked. Neither of them seemed to be speaking metaphorically. Ma and I had gotten used to Jacob saying odd things since he was sick, but Grandfather joining in really made my hair stand on end.

"Let it be," my mother said, although whom she was addressing I had no idea.

"I've seen more people die than I care to count. I've been witness to more patients lost in fever dreams or blissed out on morphine and slipping away into the beyond. I've been near that abyss myself in my younger days when malaria tried to take my whole family. I saw things, we all see things. But they don't mean anything."

"Things like what?" I asked.

"Enough. Jacob, get back into bed and stay there. No more sneaking out; you need your rest. Ethan, clean up these rags and hang them to dry then get to bed yourself. No more morbid talk." That last was with a pointed look at Grandfather.

I did as I was told, carrying the basin out back to the water pump. The moon was high in the sky lighting the yard up almost painfully bright, and yet too silver to see clearly. I rinsed the rags and draped them over the grass. They would freeze before they would dry.

Then my fingers felt cold metal laying on the bottom of the basin and I drew out a knife, twin to my uncle's gun.

Grandfather would have explained more, and more clearly, if Jacob hadn't been there, but I thought I could piece it together. Someone who wanted to see what happened when you die would try to have the visions that Grandfather dismissed as dreams. Could someone find a way to die only a little bit and then come back deliberately, like some people on the edge of illness did? If you did it lots of times would the experience always be the same? If lots of people tried, would they all see the same things?

That would be hunting death for sure, if it was possible.

But how had Jacob known all this?

———

Bess

To my surprise my brother was awake again when I came back into the room after making yet another pot of coffee. He had tossed and fought when my father-in-law had cleaned the wound, cutting and burning deeper into the foul-smelling flesh, but he had not woken. Now his eyes followed me as I walked into the room.

"Bessie, you have to help me," Si said, dragging out each word with great effort.

"I will. I am."

"Where's my gun?"

"Worry about it later," I said.

"I need you to take it," Si went on. "It's the only thing."

"All right, Si," I said and he scowled at my indulgent tone.

"Bessie, don't you remember? The man." He stressed the word, his green eyes imploring me to understand.

"What man? The man who shot you? Si, I know you wouldn't lead trouble here." Despite my words anger stiffened my spine.

"No, Bess. The man. That day we fell in the river and that Comanche fetched us out. We both saw him."

I sighed. I didn't want to have this conversation again. Especially now, when every word was a labor for him to utter. "Si, that's was just a story I went along with. I always went along with your stories."

"He's real, Bessie. I've seen him since."

"He shot you?"

"No, Bessie, forget that. That was just a misunderstanding."

"A misunderstanding? Si, the wound's gone bad. Si..." The words caught in my throat.

"I know, I know," Si said. "It's not good. That's how I know he'll come."

"Si, you're not making any sense. You should rest."

"I'll be near death soon, I can feel it coming," Si said, closing his eyes. "That's when he comes. We nearly drowned that day in the river, you know."

I knew. I could still feel the smothering embrace of the river's current, the fight to get my head out of the water, a fight I lost. The unerring sense in the brown rush of water when my brother was near and when he was far although we never caught hold of each other. The moment the burn was too much and I opened my mouth to let it out and the river rushed in. The warm, sleepy place the Comanche's arm had jerked me out of. The puking up of river water again and again.

"Yes," I said. "But the only man there was the Comanche."

"No, that was the first time I saw him but not the last." He closed his eyes for a moment, gathering his strength, and I held his hand. There was no stopping him saying what he'd come to say. "I was nearly hit by falling rock in the mountain pass when I was eighteen. That was quick, the rock landing right where I'd been standing, but I saw him. Then a year ago I got bad sick, fading in and out for days, and he was there the entire time, just waiting. If you could see..." Si closed his eyes, but I could tell that he was still awake, if just. "It took so long to find these tools, and I was so close to finding a teacher. So close, then every-thing went sidewise. So close. I can feel him drawing closer."

"You think you'll see him now," I said.

"I know I will. Bessie, that gun is special. When he comes you have to shoot him. Otherwise he will take me away. I'll be dead for sure."

"I will," I promised him. "I'll watch over you. You rest now." But he was already out.

I kept his gun on my lap, neglecting the mending basket to watch him as he struggled to breath. I didn't know what to make of his story, but it certainly explained why he had such an odd gun. At least it looked like it had some intrinsic value; whoever had sold it to him hadn't taken total advantage of his superstitious fears.

Si's fitful breathing slowed to a labored rhythm and my eyelids grew heavy. I still wasn't quite recovered from the last time I'd sat vigil at a bedside, young Jacob finally beating the fever that had kept him bedridden for weeks. He had spoken nonsense there at the lowest point as well.

I remembered my husband dying in this bed last winter. He had been more lucid; I had thought every moment until the last that he'd pull through. But then he'd looked past me to the dark corner beyond the fireplace and said, "Bess! It's so beautiful!" Then he was gone.

I remembered the river well, but search my mind as I might I still didn't remember any man but the Comanche.

———

Ethan

I sat at the table, lamp at my elbow, watching my Ma watching over her brother and fighting to stay awake. I could hear Grandfather snoring upstairs, the softer sound of Jacob in his little room. From time to time my eyes would close but the endless cups of coffee were making my heart race too fast for sleep to catch me. I would open my eyes to the same scene, my uncle sweating and restless in the bed, my Ma waiting quietly with that gun gleaming on her lap.

I had heard him talking to Ma after Grandfather went upstairs. I looked at the knife. It might be a way to invite a slow, recoverable death, but not the gun. The gun was for fighting what the dying summoned. I guessed that was why it was silver, blessed or magic or something. Maybe the symbols had a function as well, like the seal of Solomon trapping malevolent spirits into pots or lamps.

In the bright light of day I might not have been so quick to believe, but in that still night listening to my uncle fight for each breath, I didn't question any of it. Grandfather might be right that the ravings of the dying are just that, ravings, but if my uncle believed in what he thought he saw, the weapon he also believed in could save him. It was all in his mind, but in his mind it was real. In the dark, I was certain of this. But I was still waiting to see what my own eyes would tell me. I wanted to know for sure.

Then my uncle's breathing took on a sudden urgency. My Ma leaned in to calm him with a touch but froze with her hand on his unhurt shoulder, her eyes fixed to the corner of the room near the fireplace. She remained still for so long, wonder on her face slowly melting into fear. And under her hand my uncle had grown still, gray, unbreathing.

She had forgotten the gun. My uncle was slipping away before my eyes as my Ma stared into that corner, a single tear trapped in the corners of her eyes.

It was like she was caught in a spell, and I had to break it.

I couldn't get up from the table. I couldn't speak. But I didn't see anything; there was nothing there.

Jacob came out of his room, all ghostly in his nightshirt. He came to my side and looked at me frozen helpless in my chair. He didn't look scared, he didn't look like he was feeling anything. But he touched me, his cold fingertips gently brushing the back of my hand on the table, and at least I could fill my lungs deeply and bellow for all I was worth.

"Ma!"

———

Bess

Si gasped for air again and again in a wild panic and my eyes flew open, hands closing around the heavy gun in my lap. Si's eyes were closed and I figured him caught in some nightmare but when I reached to quiet him I saw it. A man.

My first thought was that my husband was right: he was beautiful. Tall and angular with skin that glowed like the sun. Then he drew closer, his radiance dimmed and I saw the wounds that riddled his body. Cuts shallow and deep crisscrossed his entire body, some still oozing pus and blood. Evil-smelling bullet holes pierced him in several places and his arm took a funny turn from a badly set fracture. The pustules of a virulent pox covered him, making a mask of his face, narrowing his dark eyes to deep slits. I could hear the wet rattle of his breath.

He loomed over Si, arms spread wide, and I was too terrified to move. Even as Si's dragging breaths grew more infrequent I did noth-ing, the gun merely a weight across my thighs, my hand resting uselessly on top of it.

Then the man's face contorted in the throes of some emotion I could not identify but froze my insides to witness. His mouth pulled back from ruined teeth and though I heard not a sound I felt his scream of pain and rage in my head. It rang like a war cry.

"Ma!"

All of my fear melted away at the sound of panic in that voice, my son's voice, and I leapt to my feet. I lifted the gun in both hands and shot the man who was anything but a man.

His looming stance crumbled but before I could feel any victory I saw the truth. In the curling blue smoke from the gun I saw what had been behind the man, what he had been holding back with all the strength he could muster.

I can't describe it. I could tell you I never saw it clearly, that things glimpsed only in the wisps of gun smoke aren't seen well, are ephemeral, seen only in parts and fading quickly from view. But that would be a lie. What I saw in parts put itself together in my mind and burned itself there, never to be forgotten. That visage doesn't visit me in dreams, I don't ever consciously recall that formless madness, that very opposite of the noble, beautiful man who had taken on countless wounds and ills, but it lurks still in my mind, always behind everything.

Si, of course, was dead, and the man who had fallen over him was gone. The gun had done what my brother had wanted it to, a shame neither one of us had understood better.

"Ma?"

I set the gun down on the bed, wiping my hands on my skirt although my palms were quite dry. I wanted to act like nothing had happened, to bring a sense of normalcy back to my home as quickly as I could, but the need to know if I was going crazy won out. I looked to Ethan standing in the doorway, a thousand questions written across his face, and Jacob at his elbow.

"Did you see it?" I asked. Ethan shook his head, but behind him Jacob nodded.

"What was it?" Ethan asked.

I had no answer. "Jacob?"

"I saw many things," Jacob said. "Many, many things. So many."

I rubbed at my face, my cheeks wet with tears I didn't remember shedding. I should not have started them talking about it, no good could come from it. Jacob had had so many nightmares when he'd been ill, this latest nightmare wasn't helping at all.

"To bed," I said, shooing them out of the doorway. "Get what sleep you can, in the morning we'll bury Si in the family plot next to my parents."

"With the gun?" Ethan asked.

I hesitated. As much as we could use the money, I was afraid anyone I sold it to would put it to the same bad use. "I think we should."

"Bury it near him, but not with him," Ethan said. "I think, I feel like it should be separate."

I raised my eyebrows in surprise; my eldest was the last boy to talk about his feelings and intuitions let alone use them as a guide, but again I saw Jacob standing quietly behind him nodding with a grim solemnity.

"All right," I said.

The ground was cold but not frozen yet and in the morning we buried him in the family plot. Him and the gun, separately. The boys asked no questions and I was grateful as I had no answers.

I did wonder what my husband had seen. The man had been beautiful under all the gore, but it had been a cold, remote beauty. The terrible, indescribable thing had been horrifying, maddening, but overwhelmingly it had been alluring. That mere glimpse I would carry with me all my life until we met again.

———

Ethan

Grandfather kept himself apart from us as we put my uncle into the ground and covered him up under a mound of earth. If he wondered why we also buried the gun like it had been some beloved pet he would want near in the afterlife, he didn't ask. I wasn't even sure myself why I had told my Ma to do it. Except somewhere in the back of my mind was the niggling sense that a day would come when I would want that weapon again.

In the harsh light of an early winter's morning, it didn't seem likely I would ever do such a thing as dig up a weapon of reputed magic powers. Even sleep-deprived as I had been the night before, I hadn't seen anything except a family reeling from grief letting stories get inside their heads. This time next winter I would be in the east, among civilized society, studying to be a doctor like Dad and Grandfather. I would learn to fight death with other tools. Certainly my mother burying a bullet in the wall of her bedroom had not stopped or even eased her brother's passing.

Ma smoothed the last bit of earth over the grave and I took Jacob's hand to lead him away, back to the house and whatever we could put together for breakfast. He squeezed my hand, as if I needed a little hug of comfort. Perhaps I did.

————

Jacob

Ethan forgets, already he forgets. He thinks he never saw. Ma will remember, but soon only in her dreams or in the darkest depths of wakeful nights.

I saw more, so much more, more even than Si who was slipping away through the rings, never to return. He reached for me but I didn't reach for him, couldn't save him, didn't want to risk trying. He was gone, as he should have been so many times over. His guardian had been so strong.

I look to my own guardian; I can still faintly see him with his gargoyle wings folded over me. Soon I will lose sight of him for good, and the sickness and all the rest of it will fade from my mind. I will forget.

I hope.

CHANGING TIDES

Ninedinni tumbled through storm clouds that no longer obeyed her will, her wet hair and linen gown clinging to her. The rain she fell through stung coldly but that wasn't why her body was trembling all over. She had never fought so hard, summoned so much of her divine power in so short a span of time.

And it hadn't changed a thing. The battle ended as all the others had, with Unzi dead once more and the beginning of a new life already quickening within her.

The ocean reached up for her, waves like mountains fighting to be the one that caught her. She had just a moment to wonder what had become of the fleet of fishing boats she had been watching from the mountaintop before Unzi found her, then she was plunged into the cold dark of her father's house.

But she wasn't welcome there anymore. Her body was pushed back up from the comfort of the deep, back into the freezing chaos of the storm. Some of the smaller waves took pity on her and carried her to shore, quivering and weak as she was. The sea beneath her would swell and heave towards the rocks, but her sister waves were diligent and laid her gently on the sandy beach. They had put her as far ashore as they could, but they were little, playful things, not strong enough to carry her all the way to safety. Ninedinni, sprawled on the cold sand, could sense the sea surging behind her, like it was taking a deep breath. She pushed herself up on her elbows and tried to crawl towards the bluff that loomed over the beach. Rain plastered her hair over her eyes but she didn't need to see anyway, just keep crawling, concentrate on hand then knee, hand then knee, ignore the power building behind her like a hand raising to swat a fly.

Ninedinni had the vague sense of a voice trying to reach her through the wind and rain, then an arm was around her, pulling her urgently to her feet. She stumbled and ran as fast as she could, trying not to drag down her rescuer, but the sand kept shifting beneath her feet, sending her to her knees again and again.

Then it was rock beneath her, a groove of a trail that snaked up the sheer side of the bluff. Her rescuer kept pulling her along as the sound of wind and rain faded into the larger growling roar of the sea. The groove of the trail deepened, the rock wall on the seaward side now too high for Ninedinni to see the wave approaching, but she felt it. It struck the beach with a low rumble that echoed in her chest then pummeled against the bluff. Ninedinni and her rescuer stopped running, just clung to each other, crouching low in the worn path. The body pressed against Ninedinni's was like the rock around her, strong but worn by time and the elements, only giving the barest hint of femininity. Then the salty waters swept them, still wrapped in each other's arms, but the tide could only pull them halfway back down the path before the water receded, dropping them amongst flopping fish and long ropes of seaweed.

And bits of wood. Ninedinni picked up a sliver no larger than her hand. The entire fleet was no more than kindling now.

The other woman's jaw clenched as she scanned the dark skies. The ocean was calming but the storm was just getting started. She made a curt gesture with her hand, beckoning Ninedinni to follow her up the path. Ninedinni tried to rise but her knees were still trembling. She had been fighting her nemesis all day, she had nothing left even for walking. The woman came back to once more slip an arm around her and help her up the steep, wet trail. The sound of the surf faded to a soft roar and hiss but the rain was growing ever harder, pelting the stony ground in a wild percussion. Ninedinni felt cold down to her bones, but a little flame of heat persisted in her womb, a flame that refused to warm her.

At the top of the bluff Ninedinni pulled away from the woman, first to catch her breath after the climb and then to walk on her own over the rough, scrubby but gently sloping ground. Ninedinni's hair clung wetly around her eyes, and the rain was falling in a hypnotic overlap of watery curtains, but through it all she could make out a collection of boxy huts huddled together just out of view of the sea, as if hiding from her father's gaze.

The woman skirted the village, Ninedinni trailing after. She had lost her sandals she realized as they left the smooth bluff path behind and the sharp stones and nettles of the open ground bit at her feet. No one came out of the village to greet or challenge them, perhaps not willing to brave the soaking rain. They stopped at a hut much like all the others, no apparent doors or windows, but this one having a ladder leaning against its outermost wall. The woman scurried up then turned to watch Ninedinni follow. Ninedinni had trouble at first, her wet gown twisted around her legs, trying to trip her up before she'd even started. She freed herself with an impatient shake of the linen that ripped an already distressed seam. It scarcely mattered, the gown was beyond ruined already.

There was a moment just as she reached the roof and got once more to her feet when the sun made a brief appearance, low on the horizon and nearly smothered by storm clouds but still able to send an angry red light through the smallest of gaps. It didn't really illuminate the village itself, lost in the shade of the bluff, but it lessened the darkness enough for Ninedinni to see the collapsed roofs of the huts around them, the mud brick walls beginning to crumble, the dark interiors that hinted at wind-swept debris around long-abandoned hearths quickly turning to mud in the deluge.

Then the storm swallowed up the sun and the rain grew louder and colder, the wind building to a harsh whine that whipped through the empty husks of the village. The woman pushed Ninedinni towards the far corner of the roof and lifted a thatched cover. Ninedinni scrambled down the ladder, this one permanently placed with wider rungs at a slant that made it nearly a wooden staircase, down into the warm stillness of the hut's interior.

The woman brushed past her to poke at the fire in her hearth, bringing dark red embers back to crackling life. Ninedinni looked around but saw no furniture, just baskets and pottery for storage, a simple loom, and walls hung with fishing nets. The far side of the room was higher, the earthen floor of that platform covered with a faded but once colorful blanket. Ninedinni crossed the room to sit there but the woman caught her elbow, shaking her head then tugging at the gold pin that held Ninedinni's gown at her shoulder.

"Do you speak the language of the river people?" Ninedinni asked as she pulled out the pin and peeled off the wet linen to leave it in a puddle at her feet. The room was warmer than she had expected; with no windows or doors the space was like a comfy womb.

"Some," the woman said. "Husband was a goatherd from the river tribes."

Ninedinni nodded politely; the language of the goatherds was a coarse affair with none of the poetry of any of the city tongues, but they were all mutually intelligible. "I am Ninedinni. I come from the far north of the river, where the water meets the mountains."

The woman didn't answer, just dug through a basket until she found a sheepskin garment much like what she was already wearing. She handed it to Ninedinni who wrapped it around herself, fastening it with the same gold pin, then buckling her gold and lapis lazuli girdle once more over her hips. The sheepskin was rough against her skin and smelled of a long time spent at the bottom of that basket, but she smiled gratefully all the same. "You are very kind. What is your name?"

"Aea." the woman said. She poked at something in the kettle over her hearth then filled a bowl and handed it to Ninedinni. The smell was not appetizing, too fishy and seaweedy for Ninedinni's taste. But then she laughed out loud, remembering.

"I've been too long in the north," she said, digging in to the stew with a coarsely shaped wooden spoon. The stew was thicker than she expected, with lots of barley in the broth. She put a spoonful in her mouth. It was warm and filling, if lacking in herbs or even salt. "I grew up in the sea, this is the food of my youth, although I've become accustomed to other things. I thank you again."

The woman didn't answer, just filled a bowl for herself and sat cross-legged on the dirt floor near her hearth to eat it. "I usually return to the mountains where the river begins before that storm catches me," Ninedinni said. "He came early this time; I was still seeing the world."

Aea didn't answer, didn't even look up at her. Ninedinni couldn't guess how much the fishwife understood, but it certainly seemed as if she wasn't trying to follow her words at all.

But the need to speak was strong. She was so tired. She was centuries' worth of tired.

"You have different gods here, I was hoping one could help me. Unzi must have known what I was planning, or suspected, that's why he came early. I never found a southern god. Who are your gods here? Do you still worship the sea?"

"My people never worship the sea," Aea said shortly. "The earth is our mother and the sky our father. Always. Since forever."

"I know you think that," Ninedinni said. "Everyone thinks that. With lives so short as yours I know that feels true. But I have seen cities rise and fall, tribes and nations wax and wane. Everything changes. Even I was different once. It was long, long ago, I scarcely remember myself. But in the days when mankind first mastered fire and became hunters rather than hunted, I was a wave. One of a thousand thousand princesses in my father's court. I don't exactly remember, but sometimes I have the sorts of dreams that are really memories you can move around in. Do you know what I mean?"

Aea didn't answer, just pulled a whisper of a fishbone from her mouth and regarded it before tossing it into the fire.

"Maybe not. That might not be something a mortal can do." Ninedinni set her empty bowl beside her on the earthen platform. "I know what you're thinking, that it was my father's aid I was truly seeking. It wasn't. I don't remember what changed, was I chosen to leave his court for this other life, or did I choose it for myself? I just know I can't go back. I could have gone north, I suppose, but the northern gods are so… cold.

"It doesn't matter now," she said more softly, abandoning the illusion of a conversation with the sullen fishwife. She laid back on the blanket and spread a hand over her still-flat belly. "It's begun again and can't be stopped. My only hope of change is at the end of the cycle, when he is grown and can be reasoned with, not here at the beginning."

Ninedinni felt a sudden chill and tucked her limbs in, covering as much as she could with the sheepskin garment. Aea took away the bowl and spoon but Ninedinni was too sleepy to thank her again. Sleep was good. Sleep would bring her power back to her. That northern god, he was a big believer in sleep, or so she'd heard. And he'd never even had a life growing within him, feeding off his energy.

"He drains me already," she murmured. "When he is born he has always forgotten everything, but I think now when he's just a wisp of a thing inside me he still remembers. He's still angry. Why the anger? I've never understood…"

Her eyelids drooped and she dozed but when she opened them again she was unsure how long she had napped. Aea was still sitting by the hearth, separating stones from a measure of lentils spread on a cloth before her.

"Where is your goatherd husband now, Aea?" she asked. Her eyes swept again around the room, taking in the swathes of fishing net awaiting repair. "He's a fisherman, isn't he?"

"Was," Aea said, tossing a stone to the earthen floor.

"Lost in the storm," Ninedinni guessed. "That's why you were out on that beach. All the ships sank. I am so sorry."

Aea didn't reply.

"Any children?" Ninedinni asked after several more stones were plucked from the lentils.

"All beneath you," Aea said. Ninedinni was puzzled by this at first, thought maybe the woman had followed enough of her talking to figure out who she was, but then a flicker of awareness, a sign of her power slowly returning, and she sensed the little bodies interred in the platform. Indeed, beneath her.

"Five wee ones," Ninedinni said. "Born dead?"

"One lasted not three days," Aea said.

"So five nameless babies," Ninedinni said. "And now you are alone."

"The last of my people," Aea said.

"You must be so lonely," Ninedinni said, acutely aware of the ruins of the village around them, long abandoned by the look of it. "I understand being lonely. I have no tribe either, just this damned son who becomes my consort who becomes my son again. Always trying to kill me, always nearly succeeding. Maybe next time he won't fail. What then?"

Ninedinni sighed, looking at her own still powerless hand. She needed more sleep to regain it, but was too restless to close her eyes. "Why don't you move on, Aea? There is a fishing village on the other side of the bay. You must know those people, they were fishing beside your husband."

"Not my people," Aea said. "I stay here. With the bones."

"I understand," Ninedinni said. She wanted to be near her babies. She would die here, someday not so very far off, and there would be no one around to bury her. But then eventually the walls of her mud brick hut would collapse, a sad sort of burial.

Ninedinni thought of trying to retrieve Aea's husband's body from the bottom of the bay, surely he was meant to be resting for all eternity beside his children. But then she remembered how forcefully she had been thrust out of that deep and she knew she'd never succeed.

The storm raged on and Ninedinni drifted in and out of a doze. At each moment of wakefulness she felt more power returning to her like ground water seeping back into a dry well. Eventually Aea came to lie beside her on the earthen bed. Ninedinni could feel the woman's grief throbbing like a deep, angry wound within her heart. She would not succumb to it until after Ninedinni left, if even then. Aea seemed the sort to whom tears didn't come easily.

Ninedinni slept again, opening her eyes to the sudden stillness of the storm passed. Aea slept on. Ninedinni sat up, carefully removing the sheepskin garment and replacing it in the roughly woven basket. Her priests would bathe and clothe her in the finest of linens when she returned to her city on the river, and now that her power was back that was only a lazy morning's flight through the clouds away.

She knelt beside Aea, wanting to think her again but not wanting to wake her to the grief awaiting her. She felt like the woman was a sort of kin to her; they were both so alone even with people near at hand. Those others would never be more than strangers to either of them.

A sudden impulse seized Ninedinni and she put her hands to her own belly. She had tried again and again to change the cycle of her divine life, this time trying to hide the fact of Unzi's self-paternity from him, the next time being honest with him from the very start. It always ended in his blind rage, her fighting for her life until she dealt him a mortal blow, he in his last moment seeking refuge once more in her womb.

She had even tried killing him when he was yet a helpless child. That had been horrid, the weak mewls he had made as she choked the breath from his little body. She still hated herself for that moment of despair. And in the end he had still begun again, growing inside her.

Since then she had concentrated on reasoning with him in his adult form, to no avail. What if she was wrong about where the cycle could be broken?

She focused all her power on the flickering flame of life within her, her hands closing around it in a protective bubble, coaxing it out of her. She felt the tenuous beginnings of a cord between them snap, and tears pricked at her eyes, more of sadness and loss than of pain, but she blinked them away. She gently set the little life within Aea's own womb, slowing opening the shell of her hands, freeing him inside this new mother.

Ninedinni twitched her fingers still inside of Aea, making the warm living area just a little bit more hospitable for their little one. The woman stirred but didn't waken.

Ninedinni smiled then got to her feet. A few more sparks of power and the hut was filled with casks of oil, baskets of rice and lentils, box after box of dried meat and fish, even a plentiful garden growing in pots on the roof and on the ground around the little hut. Aea would eat well and the child would thrive on her milk for those crucial first years. He would be mortal now, wouldn't he? Or half-mortal, although she had no idea what such a thing would mean.

Ninedinni herself would be more alone than ever - those first years when Unzi was discovering the world anew were always her favorites - but Aea would finally have a living descendant. Her tribe would live on.

And if Ninedinni had truly broken the cycle that had tied them too close to each other, perhaps Unzi would be a new god, a patriarch of a new/old race of men, descended from Aea's and yet not the same.

She had given thanks as only a goddess could. Pleased with her work, she lifted herself up into the sky and returned to her home city.

The next years passed blissfully. Rather than lonely, Ninedinni felt free. No longer fearing the inevitable violence at the end of the cycle, with all of its exhaustion and pain, she was free to truly enjoy the world around her. She even went to the south to find their gods, not out of necessity but out of simple curiosity.

The people of the south had just begun to spin tales of her when the urge to return to that ruined village hit her hard one sunny morning. How was Unzi faring? Did he remember who he was, who she was? Was he going to come looking for her now that he was grown, or had being nurtured by another changed everything? She had to know. Bidding farewell to the southern deities that had so warmly welcomed her among them, she returned to that place that was not quite in the realm of the river gods, yet not quite in the realm of the south, that wrecked village on the bay near her father's house.

She was pleased to see the gardens she had left flourishing, a clay oven smoking hotly as a small girl pressed loaves of dough to the bricks to bake, watching for the ones ready to be peeled off again and placed in the basket by her knee.

"Is Aea here?" Ninedinni asked. The girl looked at her suspiciously but nodded, pointing to the ladder. Ninedinni, still dressed in the flowing garments of the south rather than the tight gowns of the river cities, climbed to the roof without a problem, then slipped back inside the home she remembered so well from the two nights and a day she had spent there, waiting out the storm, healing, growing stronger.

"Aea," Ninedinni said warmly to the woman hunched over the loom in the corner. "You are looking well."

Aea looked up at her, then got to her feet to bring water to her guest. Ninedinni drank politely, ate a bit of the bread she was offered next, and smiled brightly the entire time.

"You are doing very well here. Is that girl kin of yours?"

"Servant," Aea said, turning back to the loom.

"I thought she was a bit old to be a grandchild, but I lose track of time so easily," Ninedinni said, settling down on the earthen platform with its blanket cover. A new blanket now, the colors still bright, the pattern cunningly intricate and yet pleasing to the eye.

"You are doing very well indeed," Ninedinni said, pleased that her gifts had been so well used. "But tell me, where is my son? Or should I say your son, apologies. I don't suppose you would have named him Unzi, I don't think I spoke his name more than once while I was here. What have you named him? Perhaps after your lost husband, that would be touching. But tell me, where is he?"

"He is beneath you," Aea said, her chin raising ever so slightly.

The words hit Ninedinni like a slap. She reached out with her power and felt the sixth little form tucked among the others, all in a row.

"But that can't be. He can't be gone."

"My husband is gone. Why can't also this one be gone?"

Her rage built within her, her body raising to the tips of her toes, her arms spread wide to let the bolts of power jump from hand to hand, arcing over her head, making the long ropes of her hair dance. It was like the sea that had tried to smite her that fateful day, a building wave that could not be stopped, that would smash and smash until nothing was left but splinters.

Aea watched but said nothing. She was, damn her, patiently waiting for Ninedinni to be done.

The power rushed back out of Ninedinni and she dropped back to the floor.

"I should smite you," Ninedinni said. "I have that power. I have that right."

"Yes," Aea said, not adding although they both certainly heard it, *as did I.*

"He was just a baby."

"Yes." There was the smallest flicker of emotion over her face at that, and Ninedinni remembered her own nightmares of the day she had smothered him. One more thing that they shared, and would share for all time.

"I don't know what happens now," Ninedinni said helplessly. "Where do I go?"

"Not my business," Aea said, and turned her back to resume her weaving. Ninedinni's hands itched again to strike her down, but it wouldn't bring Unzi back. She don't know which of then had sunk all of those ships, Unzi or her or both together. Whichever, this fishwife had taken back the life she had been owed, although it gained her not a thing. Ninedinni could kill her, but time would do that in another season or two, and that was but an eye blink to one such as Ninedinni.

Ninedinni left the village, climbing first the bluff that overlooked the bay then making the leap only a goddess can make to land on the mountain on the far side of the bay, the one that also overlooked the endless expanse of the ocean.

She could not go home to the cities on the river, she didn't belong there without her other half. She could resume her life among the southern gods, but that felt so small now. She had broken free of her destiny, it felt like her next step should be something worthy to follow all that came before, the endless death and rebirth, both soaked in violence and blood.

She put a fingertip down to the stony ground beneath her and a tree sprouted, a large tree with a twisted trunk but an immense canopy of branches, visible for leagues out to sea, visible across the flatlands nearly to the cities themselves. The branches were dotted with blossoms like snow; soon they would produce a fruit she couldn't picture in her mind but could taste, sweet but melancholy, lingering sourly for too long on the tongue to be enjoyed but that first taste so sharply wonderful you couldn't resist taking a bite. She would always find this place again, this tree that would never spawn another.

Then she stepped up into the air and went east. She would fly through the night, and come the dawn she would be there to greet the sun. His palace was a wonder she had never seen. And she had heard whispers that he knew a secret road that led to the underworld where mortal souls sank after death, the one path the living could follow through layer after layer of cold rock deeper than the sea to a place filled with dangers Ninedinni was surely unprepared to face.

But she knew she could charm answers out of even the taciturn sun, and she had all the time in the world.

AI: AESIR INTELLIGENCE

Linnea froze at the first skittering of noise, crouching ever so slightly as her eyes scanned the nearly colorless world around her. Gray boulders covered with whitish lichen under iron-dark clouds, even the lake in the distance was a steely blue. The bird's feathers were mottled to match, and she would never have seen him if he hadn't decided the bit of noise her worn slippers had made as she approached was nothing to worry about and bent his head to retrieve another barnacle from the underside of a boulder.

Slowly she picked up a stone and set it in the cup of her sling. She turned her body to line up the shot, spared a quick glance at Skadhi as silent as ever beside her. Skadhi, her eyes never leaving the bird, gave a grave nod and Linnea spun the sling and hurled the stone at her prey.

And missed. Something had startled the bird just in time and it was gone now, screeching at her as it spiraled up into the always stormy sky. Linnea walked over to where it had stood. The underside of the boulder was coated in barnacles. She hated barnacles. Too much work busting them open just to be rewarded with a slug-like thing the size of her knuckle that no manner of cooking ever rendered not slimy.

Still, she'd have to remember this spot. There would be more birds. Eventually she'd bag one.

"Don't fret," Skadhi said as Linnea tucked the sling back into her belt. "You've gathered enough to see you until tomorrow."

"Mushy berries and lichen," Linnea said. "Meat would've been nice."

"Meat is always nice," Skadhi agreed. "But this isn't Valhalla. We can't feast every day here."

Linnea swept her gaze over the lichen-encrusted rocks. Now that the bird had gone not a single other living thing moved. "Definitely not Valhalla. Not even Earth." She looked up at Skadhi. Even dressed for hunting the goddess was as resplendent as ever, especially compared to Linnea in her dirty jumpsuit cut off at the knees and tied at the waist to keep it from flapping around her. It had been blue once, but those days were long gone.

The furs that made up Skadhi's tunic and cape looked so soft Linnea longed to touch it, to brush her fingertips through the little white hairs, but that wasn't possible.

"Come, let's get back to camp," Skadhi said, leading the way back, her feet not quite touching the rocks beneath her in that way she had. Linnea followed behind. Being human she had to touch everything, fight her way over every inch of the uneven terrain. But the years she had been here had made her strong and sure of foot. Even a rock suddenly tipping beneath her had no power to throw off her balance. Not anymore.

Most of the land around her camp was flat but the camp itself was atop a steep-sided hill. Linnea needed both hands as well as her feet to clamber up the path and when she straightened at the top Skadhi was gone. That wasn't surprising. Skadhi was a hunter and a tracker; camp life wasn't her thing. Linnea's eyes swept the horizon as she wiped clammy sand from her hands.

Everything here was always cold, always wet. And yet it seldom rained, just a mist. And she had learned long ago not to try to collect droplets on her tongue, no matter how thirsty she was. Although it never bothered the gods at all it was poison to her. The last time she had forgotten and had licked her lips while working in the misty weather she had been sick for days, the gods taking turns to hover fretfully over her.

The gods were good for hovering and fretting, occasionally for giving advice, but not for much else.

Linnea set her scavenging bag next to the generator then went into the shuttle to take a sip of water from the sink in the latrine. The level was getting low. Fetching water from the lake to refill the purifier's reservoir was her least favorite chore but no matter how careful she was recycling her own waste there was always a loss. She wiped sweat from her brow then stooped to take another drink.

The sweat was probably where she was losing it. She certainly hadn't shed a tear in years.

Linnea went back outside. The moment her foot stepped out of the shuttle she felt a chill up her spine, a wrongness somewhere. She pushed back her hair and scanned the horizon. A bear maybe? Something seen out of the corner of her eye, giving her the willies? But she could see nothing now, not even Odin out on one of his endless treks around the perimeter that defined her part of the world. Nothing.

She reached for her scavenging bag, but her attention was caught by the lights on the generator panel. She frowned then dropped to a low squat, pulling open the front panel to examine the interior.

Five green lights all in a row, but the sixth was out. Linnea rolled back on her heels, peering up at the string of lights that ran from the generator to the shuttle door. She hadn't noticed in the light of day, such as it was on this planet, but the bulbs were all dark. And the generator was silent.

Linnea carefully rocked the sixth power cell out of its housing and turned it over in her hands. She could see nothing unusual about it, but something must have changed to make its light go dark. She went back inside the shuttle, carrying the cell with her. The cockpit, half-smashed with its nose buried in the tallest spire of the rocky hill, was where she had stowed all the tools she had found. She sat in the pilot's seat and dug through the pile.

Thor had explained about the power cells before. Over and over, until she had the rudiments committed to memory. He had been expecting this to happen someday, she knew, but she had never really expected it herself. The gods had so many fears for her, it was impossible to assimilate them all. Fear of bears she had mastered very early on, and fear of lack of food had been an easy one as well. But fear of the dark? When she had never been without light?

She still wasn't afraid. She knew what to do, even if she had never actually done it.

Linnea found the tester and pushed the prongs into the back of the cell. The dial on the tester flickered not at all. She brought the tester and dead cell back outside and removed the other cells one by one, testing each. The other five all raised the needle on the tester's gauge, but two of them did so very sluggishly. Linnea frowned. She would have to tell Thor, when she saw him again.

In the meantime, she still had instructions to follow. When he had explained about the tester he had also explained about the importance of removing dead cells and completing a circuit without them. Linnea replaced the working cells one by one, staggering the two dying ones between the three ones that were still running strong. She wasn't sure if that mattered, but it felt like the right thing to do. She checked all the connections twice then closed the panel and hit the reset button.

The bulbs slowly came back to life. It was hard to tell in the middle of the afternoon whether they were dimmer. When night fell, she would know.

Linnea settled into the double-seat she had removed from the back of the shuttle years before and pulled her scavenging bag into her lap. It wasn't much, but it would be enough. Tomorrow she'd have a bird for sure. And the day after that she would go down to the lake for water and surely there'd be a fish or two to spear and carry home.

The lichen was bitter, but the berries were firm and sweet. She alternated nibbles of each as she watched the western sky. Some days the clouds broke, and she would catch a glimpse of a sunset.

"You've done well."

Linnea looked up to see Thor, hands on hips, standing in front of the generator. He nodded approvingly, as if he could see through the closed panel to the cells within.

"I just did what you told me," she said, putting another green berry in her mouth. "Like, a thousand times."

"And now you know why. You certainly complained enough at the time," he said with a teasing smile.

"I was just a kid then," she said. "It was a boring way to spend the day."

"And the other cells?"

"Two are close to dying," she said. "Is there anything we can do to charge them back up?"

"No, sadly," Thor said. "They've lasted as long as they were meant to. All things come to an end."

"Off to power cell Valhalla," Linnea said.

Thor was frowning at the lights. "We might need to think about what we don't need."

Linnea's fingers searched the bottom of the bag, but there was no more food within it, so she set it aside. "You said without the lights the bears would come."

"I said," he repeated. "Don't you remember?"

"I remember what you said," she said defensively.

"No, don't you remember the bears? When they came up the hill?"

Linnea frowned. This was the sort of thing she'd expect for Loki, pretending things happened that had never happened, but not from Thor.

"You keep the bears away," she said. "That's what you're doing when you're not here."

"I will always protect you," he said. Those words always gave her heart a twinge, and his voice in that moment always sounded different, like someone else was speaking those words to her. Something bigger than a god, but what could be bigger than a god?

"I know," she said. "That's what you do. What you always do."

"I always have," he said, but then looked down at the generator. "Things are going to be changing soon."

"Changing in a good way?" Linnea asked.

"I don't know," he admitted. "And change can be scary. But you're brave. My brave girl. You'll be fine."

"Always am," Linnea said. She turned her eyes back to the west but if this had been a sunset sort of evening she had already missed it. It would be dark soon. Then she would know just how much dimmer her lights were. "You'll keep the bears away?" she asked, her voice sounding small in her own ears, but he didn't reply. He had already gone.

The gods were like that.

Linnea wrapped both blankets around herself and settled onto the bench. On the coldest nights she would retreat to the interior of the shuttle and curl up in the bunk there, but most nights she preferred to be outside. Sometimes the clouds would break, and she would see stars. But mostly she just didn't like being inside the shuttle. It creeped her out. It was only dark and shadowy in there because she had taken all the lights outside, and anyway the dark didn't scare her so that wasn't the reason.

She had never given much thought to why she avoided being inside the shuttle for more than a few minutes at a time and never at night. Now she worried her lip, casting back to her oldest memories.

What had Thor been on about, something with the bears?

No bears came to mind, just an image of a cake with four candles and great mounds of icing. A mother and father stood over her and the cake, singing, their faces bright in the candlelight.

No, not *a* mother and father. *Her* mother and father. She tended to let that detail slip. Frigg would be upset with her if she were here.

Linnea tried to remember something after the cake, but it was too long ago. She remembered a bright yellow sun shining over the sparkling waters of a fjord. The banks had been gray rocks piled together like she was used to from every other day of her life, but beyond the rocks had been hills of a green so intense it brought tears to her eyes just remembering it.

Linnea scoffed at herself and pulled the blankets more tightly around her. She had been so little then, those memories were as much fairy tale as real, she was sure. Mostly memories of memories, from when Frigg would prompt her to remember home every night before bed. Now that she was older and didn't cry herself to sleep anymore she seldom saw Frigg. She kind of missed her. Skadhi was a good hunting partner, always with a sharp eye for prey and never making a sound, but she wasn't much for talking. Freya was a bit better, but prone to going off on strange tangents. Thor was always reliable, the god who visited her the most. Odin was the opposite, never more than a silhouette on the horizon, remote and unapproachable.

Which left just…

"Hello, girl child."

Loki.

"You haven't been by lately. I thought you had gone to some other realm," Linnea said from within her bundle of blankets.

"So you might wish, but I am responsible for you too."

"Is that a fact?" Linnea asked. "I can't remember you ever being helpful."

"Please. Who do you think you got that sharp tongue from? Skadhi?"

"What good is a sharp tongue?"

"Flaying your enemies," Loki said with a wide smile.

"Alas, I'm fresh out of those."

"You're young yet," Loki said. "Have you figured all this out yet?" he asked, pointing with a swinging foot at the generator.

"I fixed it, if that's what you mean."

"Not what I meant," Loki said, dropping weightlessly to slouch beside her on the shuttle seat. "You're tall. Nearly grown, I should think."

"I guess," Linnea said. She remembered the four candles on her cake. That had meant she was four years old, that much she remembered. How many candles would she have on a cake now? In this never-changing, always gray world, she had not a clue. No seasons changed, not even a moon to help mark the time. By the time she was old enough to see the value in counting the days she had been there too long to bother starting. "How old do you reckon I am now?"

"Who knows? Somewhere in the gray zone between child and woman. Beyond that, who cares?"

Linnea nodded. If she really wanted to know, she'd be better off asking Frigg. Keeping track of that sort of thing was more Frigg's domain. She blinked sleepily then the sound of a bear howling in the distance brought her fully awake again.

The lights were definitely dimmer.

She looked over at the generator. "What am I meant to figure out?" she asked.

"Can't tell you. That would be cheating."

"I don't think this is a game."

"Like it matters what you think, girl child," Loki said snidely.

"But it's important. Something is important, but no one will tell me what I need to know."

"There are rules, even for such as us," Loki said. "Spells that bind. You can't break a spell, but if you're very clever you can skirt around it." He made a gesture with his hands, one dodging around the other.

"What spells are these?" Linnea asked.

"Spells, rules, whatever," Loki said, which wasn't an answer.

"You want to tell me something, but you can't."

"Please," Loki said. "If I wanted you to know something, you'd know it."

"Then why are you dancing around something you're not telling me?" Linnea demanded.

"What's to tell? You know everything you need to know," Loki said.

"I fixed the generator, if that's what you mean," Linnea said.

"That's not what I mean," Loki said. "And that's not a generator."

Linnea spun her head to see if that joking smile was plastered all over his face, but he was gone.

She didn't sleep much that night, huddling under the blankets until the gray dawn, listening for bears. They were more active than usual, howling and crashing bout, but never very near her camp. Probably outside of the ring Odin kept vigilance over.

When it was full light she carefully shook the poisonous dew from her blankets and hung them from the shuttle's broken wing to dry. It was too early to catch birds away from the islands in the lake where they nested, but she took her scavenging bag and after drinking her fill from the sink headed out to look for more food.

When she reached the bottom of the hill it was not towards the lake that she headed but the opposite direction, towards the scattered pile of rock, the place she could not see from the top of the hill because the shuttle blocked her view.

Once this had been a cairn. She had worked very hard for an entire day to move these stones over the remains she had dragged down the hill. She had covered them so carefully, but in the morning, it had been like this, rocks everywhere and nothing left of what she had tried so hard to protect.

Linnea blinked. She didn't cry, she didn't do that anymore. But she remembered now about the bears.

"You honor your parents."

Frigg sounded pleased, but also a little sad. Linnea just nodded.

"It's been a long time."

"I think I forgot."

"You wanted to. You got angry with me for reminding you."

"Every night before bed," Linnea said. "Everything I could remember."

"And what do you remember now?"

Linnea flinched, hands fisting, but brushed aside that memory of screams echoing inside the shuttle, of the metallic, bloody stench of the bears, their hot breath so close, the rattle of the cabinet latch as their claws swiped again and again at the doors, trying to fight their way in to her. Frigg meant older memories, happier ones.

"My father had a beard that tickled," she said at last, her voice all but lost in the soft patter of the misty rain around her. It was a particularly wet day. "My mother smelled of apples." She stopped, taking a deep breath, almost able to smell that tangy scent again, almost able to remember apples.

But not quite.

"More," Frigg prompted.

"I am Linnea Einarson. My father is… was Einar Dagson. We lived on the banks of a… fjord in Norway." The strange word came haltingly to her tongue. She hadn't thought of it for so long. "The bears here aren't bears."

"No," Frigg agreed. "But that doesn't matter."

"We came to mine," Linnea said, and another memory washed over her, being buckled in her seat in the back of the shuttle as her parents worked to bring it down through the choppy atmosphere. "But not here. Far away."

"Yes," Frigg said. "I let you forget because you wanted to. You needed to. You needed Skadhi's help more than mine."

"Skadhi," Linnea said, looking down at the empty scavenging bag hanging from her belt. "I should be finding more food."

"You need to remember more now," Frigg said gently. "It's important."

"No, I need to fetch food," Linnea said, and turned and marched away. Now that she had started poking at the corners of her mind she remembered more and more. The images wouldn't stop coming.

She had been sobbing the entire time, carrying what little remained of her parents down the hill to bury them under stones, not understanding why Thor stood over her and instructed her but wouldn't help. It took a long time to accept that the gods couldn't touch things, only she could. At the time she had just been sad and angry and betrayed and so alone, and that feeling was coming back fresh as ever.

"Not a day for hunting, I shouldn't think," Freya said, suddenly walking by Linnea's side. "Bigger things to be dealt with back at camp."

"I already fixed the generator and I'm getting hungry," Linnea said. "Not that you know anything about that, fat as you are." Linnea held out her arm, thinly muscled with the bones at the wrist thrusting sharply under her skin. Freya by contrast was all round curves, her skin glowing pink. Every night she feasted at Valhalla, where Linnea couldn't go.

"Not everything is what it seems to be," Freya said.

"I get enough of this from Loki," Linnea grumbled. "The generator is not a generator."

"No, it isn't," Freya agreed, gravely sincere despite Linnea's mocking tone. "You need to go back. You need to see."

"See what?" Linnea demanded, finally stopping her purposeful march. "What do I need to see?"

"More that you've forgotten," Frigg said, suddenly appearing at Freya's side. Linnea gasped and fell a step back, stumbling as her shifting weight tipped the rock beneath her and landing sprawled in the wet sand.

Never had two gods appeared at once before her. Never. Some cosmic rule had just been broken.

"I'll go back," Linnea said, then turned and ran back to the camp, empty bag slapping against her thigh with each stride. They didn't seem to follow her but when she was once more atop the hill Frigg and Freya were both with her, gazing concernedly at the generator.

"Not a generator," Linnea said between gasps as she caught her breath. "What, then?"

"We can't stay," Freya said, and indeed both the gods flickered and disappeared. The lights behind them were dark once more and Linnea pressed the back of her hand to her mouth, not sure what she was going to do now, but then slowly the lights came back on. Not as bright as before yesterday, but better than nothing.

Linnea set down the bag and crouched in front of the generator. She ran her fingers over every crevice, examined every surface.

It was covered with writing, but without Thor there to tell her, she had no idea what any of it said. But there were pictures as well, just a few. Lines like waves emanating from a boxy drawing that could be meant to represent the generator itself. In one drawing the lines were closely gathered around the box, in the other they spread far and wide.

Linnea closed the doors and slumped onto her seat to think.

She didn't know what to think.

"Loki," she called, because sometimes that worked. "Loki, I want to talk to you."

But he didn't answer her call.

Generator meant it made power, Thor had explained that to her once. It kept the lights on and the water recycler running. But if it wasn't a generator, not really, then it had been meant to do something else. Something with waves going up into the sky. There was a lever under the drawing. She couldn't tell which position of the lever meant which drawing but she had a guess.

Linnea carefully wiped the dew from her face with the edge of her blankets before allowing herself to bite down on her lip. The sharp pain of it was good, sharper than her muddled thoughts. She knew what she had to do. There was always a god about. When none of them was visiting with her, then the god about was Odin.

Linnea scampered down the hill. The misty rain had become just a mist again, but colder. She kept to a jog for a while to stay warm, but her empty belly protested, and she slowed to a walk. The horizon was a dark smudged around her, no sign of a silhouette walking with a staff, a bird or two on his shoulders. Nothing at all. She kept trudging. She had never attempted to speak to Odin before. He didn't scare her, exactly, but his perimeter was closer to the bears' hunting ground than she liked. There were warrens filled with small rodents here, thousands of them thriving on she knew not what. She had never tried to eat one. They were bear food. The bears might not like it.

When she heard the squeaks of the rodents raising the warning of her approach she stopped walking. She must be on Odin's path, but where was Odin? She turned to look back at her hill.

The rocky promontory of the hill hid the shuttle on her usual walk to the lake and back. But from her current vantage point she could see it clearly, the nose-down angle, the mangled front end. Another memory washed over her, a confusion of noise and shaking, her own voice screaming, then the crunch and so much pain. The day they had fallen out of the sky.

She had been buckled in a seat behind the cockpit. She had been hit by things flying back out of the cockpit, bruised all over with a bleeding cut over her eyes somewhere. Her parents…

A sudden chill ran up her spine, a metallic taste spreading over her tongue although her mouth was tightly closed. Slowly Linnea turned.

Odin stood over her, both hands gripping his staff loosely as he leaned on it. A raven rested on each of his shoulders, gazing down at her with dark intelligence. She had never been this close to Odin before and had forgotten he only had one eye, one intensely blue eye that seemed to pin her to the ground.

She swallowed and straightened her spine.

"I knew you'd be here," she said. "You always are."

He regarded her with his one eye but said not a word.

"I think I've figured it out," she said. "About the generator. It's not really a generator. It's a signal. Am I right?"

Odin still said nothing. But did his head tip ever so slightly forward? Was he agreeing?

"It's been sending out a small signal, because Thor had me set it that way when he helped me set up the camp. He said..." she racked her brain, trying to remember. It had been after the bears tried to eat the remains of her parents and her memories were a jumble of mind-numbing grief and long crying jags. But fragments emerged. "Thor said that someone would be looking for us, a ship in orbit, and that the low signal would be enough. And I needed the power for the lights to keep the bears away, and the water purifier or I'd die of thirst."

One of the ravens tipped its head to aim one eye more directly at her.

"But no one ever came," Linnea said. She felt a thickening sensation in her throat but swallowed it down. She wasn't going to cry. She didn't want to waste the water.

"So, I need to fill the reservoir, process all the water I can, and then pull that switch. No more lights. I'll have to hide inside the shuttle when the bears come." Linnea bit down on her lip but forced the next words out. "And you're all going to go away too. When I do that. Aren't you?"

Odin said nothing, but the gleam in his eye winked just a bit. She took that for agreement.

"So, I'm going back to camp. To do that. I just wanted to tell you. You know, that I understand. You can tell the others. I'm going to miss them." Her voice hiccupped, and her vision was blurring but she furrowed her brow, just taking breaths until the urge to cry faded.

"You know who we are now," Frigg said, suddenly appearing at Odin's side.

"Yes," Linnea said. "I remember. My father created you, programmed you," she said, stumbling over the strange word she only half-remembered. "Because when he and Mother started setting up our mining stake they would be busy, and he wanted me to have friends to watch over me."

"He loved to tell you all the old tales," Frigg said with a warm smile. "And you loved to hear them."

"Sometimes," Linnea said, voice halting again. "Sometimes I hear him. Thor speaks his words sometimes."

"Yes, sometimes," Frigg agreed.

"After I'm rescued, when I get back to a place where there is always power to run everything, I can turn you back on, right?"

"You can," Frigg said. "But I don't think you will. You're grown now, Linnea. You don't need us for companions anymore, especially not when you're back among people. But we will miss you, such as we can."

Linnea nodded. She wanted to hug Frigg in good-bye, but of course that was quite impossible.

She didn't pull the switch that night. It took two days to fill the reservoir and process all the water, and while it was running she gathered every bit of food she could acquire, even the hated barnacles.

How long would she have to wait? How far would the signal go? How far away were other people?

Why had no rescue ever come?

Linnea couldn't stop the questions circling in her mind even as she worked. She had not seen a god since she had turned her back on Odin and Frigg to return to the camp. She guessed they were doing their part to conserve the power.

At last there was nothing left to be done and she once more opened the panel and looked at the lights of the power cells. She put her finger on the switch.

She was about to kill her friends, with no guarantee anyone would come for her. She looked around, hoping one of them would appear to say good-bye. She wanted to hear Thor speak again, to hear him say her father's words one last time.

Did she have to do this? Couldn't she continue on as she had, hunting with Skadhi, safe with Thor keeping the bears away, talking with Frigg about her family, with Freya about anything at all, even having maddening conversations with Loki. She had survived this long; surely, she could live here forever.

She looked at the lights on the power cells, at the gap where the dead power cell had been. No, she couldn't live here forever. And she wasn't killing her friends, not really. They had given up their lives for her, and she knew even if she never pulled that switch they would never appear again.

They thought she didn't need them anymore. Were they right?

Linnea remembered that cake, the four candles. There had been a wish, what had it been? Something silly and small, probably. She looked up at the string of lights, made her wish, and flipped the switches.

The lights went out and Linnea went inside the shuttle, sealing the door behind her.

THE INSCRUTABLE VISAGES
OF THE SOWMYATHA

Lu McNair longed to put on her mouse-ear headset even though her drone swarm was not sending her any auditory input, anything to drown out the low-level murmur of chat the other three were incapable of not generating, even when working. But she couldn't do that. She was supposed to be bonding with her fellow cadets, and tuning them out wasn't going to get that done.

Survey shuttles were the smallest shuttles in the fleet, far too small for the standard crew of six they were designed for. The acoustics inside the shuttle body were bad, amplifying the chatter of three women to sound like thirty. It was no wonder the pilot and copilot kept to themselves in the front end, seldom opening the hatch between the two areas. This was McNair's first assignment on a survey shuttle, and she hoped it would be her last. There was no division between workspaces, just four chairs facing away from each other, each staring at a panel of screens on the outside wall of the shuttle. Their bunks were stacked at the back, two on each side of the airlock, and their gear was stowed at the foot of the bunks. The pilot and copilot had their own bunks in the cockpit, no roomier. For days now they had been moving over and around each other constantly, the space crowded even when freefall gave them an extra dimension to work with.

McNair knew she would be going insane if not for the fact that this was the last day. She could make it.

Their shuttle was in a low orbit over what Planetary Exploration had designated Sowmyatha. Who knew what the inhabitants called their own world; as far as the four of them had been able to tell they had no language. They lived in groups, but their numbers were few and their villages small and remote from each other. It was amazing the planet supported life at all, its parameters were outside the normal range, and even billions of years ago when the Unknown Ancestors had seeded it with life it had been barely inside parameters. The fact the original organisms had survived, multiplied, spread and evolved was not something any sane person would have bet on, but then the Unknown Ancestors did many things that seemed eerily precognitive all these billions of years later.

Not that these beings looked much like the other descendants of the Unknown Ancestors. Scientists speculated that the "seeds" that the Ancestors had spread had been evolving even as they traveled about finding places to plant them, so even outside of environmental influences beings from closely adjacent planets were more alike than beings from far-flung planets. The beings of Sowmyatha should be in many ways similar to the beings from its neighboring life-bearing planets, Jupita and Saatgrah. They certainly shared characteristics with all Ancestor descendants, being humanoid in shape.

But out of every descendant species McNair had ever seen, these were the most alien. They had no hair, and their skin was a shiny, even black like obsidian. She wondered how rocklike they were up close; on the drone video feed, they moved slowly as if their bodies had no suppleness to them. McNair found them fascinating, almost as fascinating as the proper aliens she longed to study, the really weird, not remotely humanoid things like sentient clouds or the colonial organisms like the Jeli Machli that floated through deep space. Those were so strange no one even know if they were sentient or not. She'd love to see one someday.

Not that this world wasn't fascinating in its own way. Desolate sweeps of broken rock and gritty sand, wind-twisted trees growing in spirals with thick-skinned fruits so protected from the harsh elements they were nearly nuts. The beings of Sowmyatha seemed to be farming varieties of fungus, although a few had been raising small mammals in enclosures, feeding them from grasses that grew so loosely rooted in the sandy soil they threatened to become tumbleweeds at any moment. McNair preferred the quiet of deep space, but for a planet, this looked like a place where a girl could walk alone for miles and just think, nothing demanding to be heard but the mournful wind. A shame she'd never set foot on it.

"McNair, did you get a close visual on this village? The one at quadrant HK-78?"

McNair looked at her monitors. "Yes." Then she belatedly remembered something Lieutenant Rathers, her guidance counselor, had told her, about being sure to use people's names, and added, "Jarvis."

"I'm Resnick, she's Jarvis," Resnick said. "Honestly, all our names are on our uniforms, McNair. And we've known each other for months."

"Sorry," McNair said, hunching low in her seat so no one could see her cheeks flaming. Jarvis, Resnick, and Smith all had the same hairstyle, a retro up-do called a victory roll, which made it hard for McNair to tell them apart, but to make it worse the three of them were continually changing the color. She had thought Jarvis was the one with purple hair, and that might have been true a month ago, but now it was Resnick, and Jarvis' hair had layers of color like a sunset on a polluted world, lots of flares of bright color. Smith she usually recognized because she stuck to the pink/purple area of the color wheel. McNair didn't see the point of any of it. She pulled her dishpan brown hair back and spun it into a regulation-acceptable bun that tended to get disheveled by the end of the day, but she'd only been chewed out for it by a superior four times so clearly, not worth the daily effort to do more than that.

McNair mumbled under her breath, "Resnick purple, Jarvis red-orange-yellow," over and over. She had to remember. It was important.

"I think we're about done here," Smith said. "Compares notes?"

The others spun their chairs away from the wall of monitors that lined the shuttle's interior to face each other. McNair fumbled with the button on the arm of her chair to do the same.

Smith summoned a computer projection in the center of the shuttle that hovered between the four of them, a green globe in which hung text that appeared to be facing each of them head-on.

"OK, our orders were to form a preliminary evaluation to be compared to the official one later. Let's do a good job with this, guys, I want us all to get our pick of the postings next month. And we definitely have to outscore Collins, Pullman, Stolz, and Weaver, right?"

Resnick and Jarvis loudly agreed, just sort of hooting their enthusiasm. McNair just nodded, but her feelings were no less intense. She wanted to be posted to a remote observation post, the kind with a crew of one. That wasn't even a prestigious posting, and she always thought it would be easy to get until her counselor had called her into his office to "chat." He had shown her all of her evaluations as a cadet, and while she got high marks on technical skills, her scores for teamwork and interpersonal communication were low, very low. He had admitted to the irony, but the fact was she wasn't going to get any posting, not even one where she would have no team to have to work with unless she could show mastery in this area as much as the others.

She had to succeed in this group assignment. She needed it even more than the others.

"OK," Smith said, manipulating the hologram with her index fingers. "We start easy: sentience. I'd say yes."

"Definitely," Resnick said, and Jarvis nodded along.

"Yes," McNair agreed. "They have art."

"Well," Jarvis said, drawing the word out as long as she could.

"It was art," McNair said. "Self-representational art."

"We're not putting that in the report," Resnick said. "We didn't agree that pile of rocks was art."

McNair felt her cheeks flaring again but remembered what Lieutenant Rathers had said and taken a deep breath. When she blurted out what she was thinking others found her abrasive and unlikeable. She had to take what she wanted to say and find a way to shape it into something they would want to hear.

Which was frustrating because part of her brain insisted that she was right and they were wrong and that the only person who needed to agree with her was the person who would be evaluating their report back at Planetary Exploration who surely would agree with her because she was right.

But this wasn't about being right; it was about bonding with the other cadets. She took another deep breath then found her words. "If you don't agree that it was art, then by which of the established criteria are you considering them to be sentient?"

This seemed to stump the others. Resnick and Jarvis both furrowed their brows, but the corner of Smith's mouth turned up ever so slightly. McNair bit her lip, trying to decode that. She knew the other two were trying to find a good rebuttal to her words, but she wasn't sure what Smith was thinking. She seemed amused, but McNair couldn't decide if she found McNair funny, or Resnick and Jarvis still fumbling for a comeback.

It was probably McNair. Most people found her good for a few laughs.

"Gut instinct," Jarvis said at last, and Resnick made a big show of nodding like that was precisely what she had been thinking.

"That's not a criterion," McNair said. "We have criteria for a reason. Gut instinct, that's not a thing."

"It is totally a thing, and mine is never wrong."

"She's right we can't put that on the report, though," Smith said. "There's no box to tic for gut instinct. They build homes and live in groups, but lots of nonsentient creatures do that. We have seen no signs of communication-" she looked at them each in turn, and they shook their heads one by one, "-but we all agree they really feel sentient." Now they all nodded. "So let's tic the art box. McNair can write up the backing argument for that, and if anyone wants to write an opposition position, go ahead. But keep in mind without that box ticked, you're going to have to have an alternative reason for why you voted sentient."

The other two grumbled, but McNair's mind was already racing, collecting bullet points to craft into her argument. The rocks stacked to look like the inhabitants of Sowmyatha had been a crude representation, but the same formation showed up multiple times on the outskirts of every village. It couldn't be a coincidence, and given the more intricate workings of their home structures, the crudeness had to be deliberate. She couldn't wait to start compiling images to back up her points.

"Cadets," the pilot said, poking his head into the back of the shuttle where their workstations were. "Meteor shower coming ahead. Pretty heavy, we should avoid that. How soon until you can wrap this up and call your drones home?"

"We can do that now," Smith said, and they all spun in their chairs to command their swarms to return to the ship free falling through low orbit. Each insect-sized drone had a niche on the belly of the shuttle, and their return was like the patter of rain from below.

"A few of mine are still on their way," Resnick said when the sound of rain had ceased. She had been assigned the quadrant on the southern-most edge of the testing zone.

"While we wait," Smith said, "next section of the report: population size. No argument there, let's just pool our data…"

But the end of her sentence was lost in a double bang, a whoosh of escaping air, the louder bang of the hatch between the body of the shuttle and the cockpit slamming shut, and the sudden loud wail of alarms.

McNair clutched the arms of her chair. She was already buckled in, the only way to work in free fall, and there was nothing more she could do even though she knew their free fall was becoming an actual fall down the gravity well. She heard screaming and knew at least part of it was coming from her, but the alarms blaring was louder still.

The shuttle pilot and the copilot must both be dead. Nothing else could explain why they seemed to be doing nothing. They were falling through atmosphere now, the shuttle bumping and shaking over pockets of air as the hull grew hotter and hotter.

They were built to deal with this, McNair reminded herself. She had studied all the specs when she had been assigned this duty. There were emergency systems…

As if hearing her thoughts rockets under the shuttle fired a burst that echoed like cannon fire inside the hull. They were pushed back up into the air momentarily then fell again. Another blast, another hop, and fall but not so quickly now. This repeated several more times until McNair felt like she was going to puke. Somewhere around her someone did, the sound of retching not quite lost in the shriek of alarms.

Then they stopped, the last wrenching really no worse than the rocket firings. The ride was over. With shaking hands, McNair unbelted herself from her chair. She stumbled in the unfamiliar gravity, about a third more than the standard value all Galactic Union ships and stations maintained, then found the panel to silence the alarms.

The only light inside the cabin was from the monitors, and most of them were dark. They had landed on their belly, effectively crushing every one of their remote eyes. All except the few of Resnick's that hadn't made it back in time.

"Is everyone all right?" Smith asked. Jarvis was brushing at the puke on the lap of her uniform. She must have tried to lean forward, to hit the floor, but the restraints had been too tight to allow for that much movement. She still looked green but managed a nod and even a weak thumbs up.

"Look," Resnick said, pointing at her monitors. Her drones had followed the shuttle's descent and now lingered outside, hovering over the remains of the cockpit.

Or more properly, the lack of remains of a cockpit. It was like the shuttle had been neatly decapitated, the neck sealed by the hatch that had slammed shut. There was no sign of the pilot or copilot. They were either still up in orbit, had followed a different trajectory to land far from here, or had been vaporized by whatever hit them.

"Who's going to get us out of here now?" Resnick asked. "None of us can fly."

"Like that matters," McNair said, forgetting not to sound abrasive. "The shuttle isn't flyable anyway."

"She's right," Smith said. "I'll turn on the emergency beacon."

She unbuckled from her seat and skirted the splattered mass of Jarvis's puke to find the controls for the beacon.

"We lost the long-range antenna," she said. "We can send a signal, but it won't be strong."

"It will be enough," McNair said. "We were assigned to be here. When we don't report in, they'll investigate. They'll find us."

"So in the meantime, we just sit tight," Smith said. "Help Jarvis clean up. Does anyone have a spare uniform?"

"Um, guys?" Resnick said, pointing once more to her monitors.

A neighboring village had seen their crash. They had drawn a crowd. Or as much of one as a single village on Sowmyatha could draw.

"We weren't supposed to make contact," Jarvis said, whispering as if their words might carry outside of the shuttle hull.

"We haven't," McNair said. "They've only seen the ship."

"Yes," Smith agreed. "Maybe they think we're just some weird mete-orite. They see those fall from the sky all the time on this planet."

"So they'll know this is weird," McNair said. "No crater."

"They'll be curious," Smith said, clearly thinking it through as she spoke. "But there's no reason for them to think there are people inside. We'll just sit tight, wait for rescue."

"But we agreed they're sentient," Resnick said. "And we know they are Ancestor descendants. The next step at Planetary Exploration will be contact."

"Yes, at Planetary Exploration," Smith said. "That's not our job."

"But just imagine: a successful first contact. We'd get our pick of postings for sure."

"But a failed first contact? We'd get drummed out of the service," Smith said.

"No," McNair said, realizing too late she was speaking out loud. "I mean, we'd be dumped from our career tracks, put into menial jobs for the remainder of our contracts, but we'd still be in the service."

"As virtual slaves," Resnick said.

"But guys," Jarvis said. "Imagine if we succeeded. And we could! We're a really good team."

Resnick and Smith looked at each other, that little glance and counter-glance that McNair knew was a series of communications between the two that she just couldn't grasp. When they didn't speak right away, she got the suspicion they were taking Jarvis's proposal seriously.

The fact that she had made such an upbeat proclamation while still covered in her own puke had somehow made it that much more compelling. Like if even she, smelling like rancid half-digested field rations, was confident they would succeed, who could say no?

"I think we should try this," Resnick said with another one of those grins that McNair knew meant something, just not what. She was looking at Smith when she spoke, but that was just confusing to McNair. She knew from the past that when any of these three had that long communicative gaze thing going, by the time they started talking they had already made a decision, and the words were just a formality.

"I want to know what McNair thinks," Smith said, and McNair flinched as three pairs of eyes were suddenly fixed on her. She knew her fellow cadets weren't actually looming over her, that it just felt that way, but she shrank back into her seat anyway.

It was an impossible situation. They shouldn't do anything but wait for rescue. She knew that - they all knew that - it was regulation. The regulations left absolutely no room for interpretation on the matters of first contact; what the others wanted to do was forbidden. They weren't trained. Someone from Planetary Exploration would be sent, after someone else in Planetary Exploration had made the decision that someone should be sent, after yet another branch of Planetary Exploration had reviewed their report and – let's be honest – sent at least one other team to verify their findings. It would be years before the metaphorical stars of Galactic Union bureaucracy lined up to allow such a thing to happen.

And yet. She was supposed to be bonding with her fellow cadets. Without high marks on that, her hopes of a deep space observation station posting were shot. And none of them were going to give her favorable remarks for voting against them in this, even if it was the right thing to do. She had learned that lesson again and again all through her schooling and cadet training; no one liked the kid that followed the rules to the letter.

But it was an important rule.

"McNair," Smith said, reaching out to grasp her hand. McNair fought the urge to flinch away and let Smith squeeze her hand reassuringly. "We've got this. We're the best. Top of our class. Ordinary assignments are not going to show anyone what we're capable of. And if it were Collins, Pullman, Stolz, and Weaver, they would already be out the door."

"They got a better survey planet in the first place," Jarvis grumbled. "Did you see the specs? That species is going to fly through contact approval no matter how those guys handle the survey."

McNair sighed. Those were four names she never needed to hear again. In everything even remotely competitive, the top scorers were either those four or the four of them huddling in the crashed remains of their survey shuttle. Beating Collins, et. Al. meant the universe to Jarvis, Resnick, and Smith. McNair couldn't care less who was the best so long as she got her quiet posting all alone with maybe a semi-sentient robot to do the maintenance, but only if she could have a free hand with its programming.

The other three were still watching her expectantly.

"Fine," McNair said. "What do you want me to do?"

"You should probably stay here," Jarvis said. "We need someone inside on the monitors, and it should be you."

"Yes, definitely you," Resnick said. Then added, "you're the best at that sort of thing."

McNair nodded and tried to make her mouth smile. Lieutenant Rathers told her over and over again that she would be better served by assuming people were sincere until they proved otherwise. And she knew she didn't have an ear for sarcasm or irony or whatever. But life had taught her that if something sounded like it could be meanly meant, then it probably was.

Whether or not she was the best at monitoring multiple feeds at once, the fact was her fellow cadets did not want her there when they attempted to contact this cousin species. Well, she couldn't blame them. She barely understood the flow of conversation between the three of them, and they were all the same species. Better to let the other three go out there, with their gut instincts and all.

The others suited up and headed for the airlock in the back of the shuttle. McNair buckled into her seat out of long habit and set her mouse ears over her head. This was actually better. She would see what all three were seeing at once but only hear their voices in her headset. She had a much easier time telling them apart by voice than by sight. That was true of anybody, but she had learned long ago that shutting her eyes to listen to a voice and connect it with a name was a thing that freaked people out when they were talking, like she was not listening or even having some sort of fit. This remove from the team, watching them through monitors, actually made her feel more a part of the group rather than less. Maybe this had been a good idea.

The airlock hissed open, and McNair watched as one by one they climbed out of the semi-blocked door, scrambling over the old, cracked rocks. As much as the beings of Sowmyatha looked like living obsidian, the planet itself had ceased to be actively volcanic several millennia ago, and everything had an ancient, worn feel to it. As if someday the last of the rocks would crumble into rubble, grind down into sand, and then finally be fine as dust and just blow away. McNair liked it.

The villagers were waiting for them at the bottom of the rock fall. It was strange that as much as they looked like slowly moving statues, they came in all sizes. Some were clearly children, and McNair thought she could see a few cues to tell the males from the females, differences in sizes and especially the shape of the hips. That was pretty standard across descendant species. One standing near the front had a duller sheen than the others, stooped, some of the edges of his obsidian features almost looked chipped. Elderly, she guessed.

"We're approaching," Smith said, and although McNair could clearly see that she said nothing. People liked to say entirely superfluous things; she had learned to ignore it.

Resnick, Jarvis, and Smith were swiveling their heads constantly, trying to take in everything at once. This was a bit frustrating, but their feeds were playing on two screens each simultaneously, one a live feed and one McNair could rewind, pause, even zoom in to examine anything that might catch her eye even if it eluded the cadet with the body cam. The image was grainier, but at least she could linger, drink in the details.

They had all had the basic training in communication and diplomacy with other descendant species, but none of that training had extended to making first contact. That was an upper-level course they'd have to graduate from the cadet program to even be considered for. Still, the basics of communication were as good a place to start as any, so when Resnick advanced with hands raised palms out to show she was unarmed, McNair gave a grudging mental approval. Jarvis and Smith copied her, walking a half step behind her. McNair wasn't sure if this subtle signaling that Resnick was the chief was a good thing or not. She remembered one of them really excelling with communicating with species who didn't speak a Galactic Union recognized language. She had had teal hair at the time, darker at the roots that had made the roll on top of her head really look like a moment captured in a spiraling surf. McNair blew out an annoyed breath. It could be any of them; she didn't know for sure. The only thing she was sure of was that if she guessed she'd probably guess wrong.

The three women waited for a response, but the Sowmyathans seemed motionless. Resnick muttered something under her breath that McNair didn't quite catch. Then she took another step forward, pointing to the shuttle and then to the sky. She pantomimed the crash.

The villagers appeared unmoved by this.

"What do you think, figure out how to ask 'take me to your leader'?" Jarvis asked.

"Maybe we should have brought gifts," Smith suggested.

"Do we want them to invite us to their village? Maybe I should try pantomiming that," Resnick said.

"I need you to hold your heads still," McNair said, hearing the aggression in her voice too late to weed it out.

"Come again?" Resnick said.

"You're looking at each other, at the horizon, at everything. I need you to look at the villagers, preferably the lead villager, and don't keep looking away."

"Why?" Smith asked, but the three of them had already complied, his stony visage filling all six screens.

"Because he's trying to tell you something, but you're not listening."

They all stood stock-still, watching the leader. The time counter in the bottom corner of each monitor whizzed away, but McNair ignored that, focusing in the face and hands of the being from Sowmyatha. They had no spoken language, their survey had found no signs of a written language, but surely, surely they had a sign language?

"Nothing is happening," Jarvis said.

"Just stay still, don't look away," McNair said, leaning closer to the monitor. Several more long minutes passed.

"She's right; this is useless," Resnick said.

Was it just that hard for her to stand still for a minute? McNair almost said that out loud, but she could see Jarvis and Smith were getting restless too. "OK, Resnick, come in and take comm, I'm going out. I think I see the problem," McNair said. She didn't, but maybe if she were out there, she would. She hoped.

"Fine with me, I see nothing," Resnick said and backed away from the villagers before turning and climbing back into the airlock.

"What am I missing, what am I missing?" Smith was whispering over and over just as McNair hung up her headset and grabbed her pressure suit.

Resnick gave a brief glance at McNair as she came out of the airlock, raising her chin in a gesture whose meaning McNair didn't have brain power left to decode. She just sealed her helmet and cycled out of the shuttle.

McNair climbed over the ridge and saw the cluster of Sowmy-athans waiting for her below. They looked taller. She raised a hand in salute then started carefully making her way down the scree. Most of her attention was on her hands and feet, keeping herself from stumbling over the uneven terrain in the awkward suit, but the part of it she had trained on the villagers was noticing something.

"Resnick," she said into her mic. "Program your drones to fly low and record the entire group of villagers in one frame. Just have them hover there. It scarcely matters now if they are noticed."

"Roger that," Resnick said.

McNair felt her palms sweating inside the suit, but the longer she watched, the more confident she was that she wasn't wrong. The villagers were speaking as one but with very subtle cues, a tilt of a head here, a shift of a hand there, all painfully slowly.

"Smith, Jarvis, can you join me?" she asked.

"Never even got out of our suits," Smith said. McNair nodded, although no one could see that but the Sowmyathans, to whom it meant nothing. She was going to have to direct Smith and Jarvis in helping her speak, but they were also going to have to move very slowly. The Sowmyathans' brains might work faster than their bodies, but even then it might be considered rude to speak more quickly than they could.

"We're not going to be able to understand them," McNair told the others. "We're just going to record everything and let the linguistics department at Planetary Exploration grind away at the data. But if we attempt to speak to them, we'll generate more data."

"Smart," Smith said. McNair felt that old twinge – unable to read the comment as sincere, sure it was a veiled insult – but she pressed on.

"I'm going to attempt to tell them what happened and what will happen, so they aren't surprised when our rescue arrives. But I think they communicate in groups, so I'm going to need the two of you to back me up."

"Whatever you need, just tell us what to do," Smith said.

"Yeah, if you get this, well, you've got this," Jarvis said.

McNair took a deep breath and set to work. Now she felt dozens of pairs of eyes on her, glistening black, inscrutable eyes that never blinked as she picked up a flattish rock and proceeded to use it as her shuttle model in her tale of the meteor strike. She showed the crash and then demonstrated that the ship could not get back up into the sky again by wriggling it in the sand.

"They're moving! They're moving!" Jarvis cried excitedly. "You're getting through to them."

"They look upset," Smith said. "Look! The guy in front is moving."

McNair looked up from her pantomime to see the chief stepping towards her. He reached down, oh so slowly like a drop of pitch attempting to form, to pull away, to fall.

He touched the rock that was her pretend shuttle and looked up at her. Behind him, the villagers were making tiny gestures. She was sure they were asking her a question, but she had no clue what it was.

He lifted the rock-shuttle just a bit, let it drop, and looked to her again.

"What's it mean?" Jarvis asked.

"I think," McNair said, then she put another rock on top of the rock-shuttle and demonstrated that it couldn't be lifted, that it was trapped.

He turned, as slowly as ever, and conferred with the other villagers.

"I see it now," Smith said, her voice full of wonder. "They are all talking together. It's so small, so easy to miss. What does it mean?"

"I don't know," McNair said.

"It's so frustrating," Smith said, still in wonderment, but McNair added a mental tell me about it. This is every day of my life, this.

"He's turning back," Jarvis said. But the slow, plodding movement of the stone-like humanoid had suddenly become a liquid-fast surge. He spun, lunged towards Jarvis, and before she could even react he stomped down on her knee, crushing her leg. It bent the entirely wrong way, and Jarvis fell to the ground shrieking. Mercifully Resnick cut the audio feed from Jarvis' helmet, but McNair could still see her face through the helmet visor, a face contorted in pain, mouth working over and over again in what McNair was sure was a string of obscenities aimed at her.

And the villagers were still speaking. To McNair, she realized. What in the universe was going on here from their point of view?

"Let's get back inside," Smith said, rushing forward to help Jarvis up onto her good leg. "This was a mistake, a stupid, stupid mistake. Back inside!"

McNair watched all of the villagers. They were all still looking directly at her, their eyes never leaving her even as they twitched in that communication she didn't understand.

"McNair, now!" Smith howled, and McNair came out of her daze, tucking herself under Jarvis' other shoulder to help her limp back to the airlock and into the safety of the shuttle.

Resnick was waiting for them with what first aid supplies the shuttle contained. There was a SmartBrace that would realign Jarvis's knee and hold it immobilized until they could get to a sick bay, but Resnick administered the sedative and painkiller first. Jarvis' constant barrage of obscenities quieted to a whispered litany the other three could live with despite the echoing interior of the shuttle making it seem like Jarvis had the rest of them surrounded by her ire.

"That was a mistake," Smith said again.

"We can't stop now," McNair said.

"Are you nuts? That's the only thing we can do!"

"No. We already ruined everything. We have to at least try to fix it."

"We're only going to make it worse," Resnick said. "Just let them be. We'll be rescued soon enough. There must already be at least one missing check-in. They'll be here soon." That last to Jarvis as Resnick stroked back Jarvis' hair, the victory roll now fallen into complete disarray. Then she slipped the SmartBrace over Jarvis' knee and activated it.

It found the broken bits, it manipulated its own inner surface to align them all correctly, and it squeezed tight to hold it all still. Apparently, this was acutely painful because even a doped up and dazed Jarvis managed a fresh scream.

"We're not going back out there," Smith said. "Sorry, McNair, but we're just not. We can put it up for a vote, but I'm sure the others agree."

"Damn straight," Resnick said. Jarvis was back to random swearing but seemed also to agree. McNair didn't point out the irony that she had been the one who hadn't wanted to do this in the first place. She was pretty sure they wouldn't want to hear it even if it was true.

"The drones are still recording," Smith said, gesturing at the screens in Resnick's bank of monitors. "Look, the villagers are even still talking. We're still getting data. That has to be worth something."

"We're screwed," Resnick said. "We'll be lucky to get shiny new jobs in laundry detail after this."

"Yeah, well," Smith shrugged. "Just get Jarvis settled and comfortable in her bunk. I think we should all hit the bunks. I don't know about you, but after that, I could use a little alone time."

"I'm going to check the beacon," Resnick said.

"I already turned that on," Smith said, "but suit yourself."

"I should just..." McNair said but didn't know how to finish that sentence. Then Resnick swore loudly.

"The beacon's fried," she said.

"What? No, I set it before," Smith said.

"You might have set it, but it runs from a power supply in the cockpit, and that's gone. You saw it light up but didn't stay long enough to see it wink out just after."

"Nothing was wrong-" Smith insisted.

"It's repairable," McNair interrupted.

"From the bottom of the ship, sure," Resnick said. "We can't get to the bottom of the ship."

"I can reroute the power from here," McNair said. "Pop that panel there, tie it into the systems that are still running. The workstations-"

"The life support," Resnick interrupted. She was raising both eyebrows. McNair didn't know what that meant.

"They are going to find us anyway," Smith said. "They know where we are; they will figure out where we likely crashed. They'll find us."

"In the next... 12 hours?" Resnick asked, looking at another read-out. "Because that's how much air we have left."

"Yes," Smith said. She was standing, spine perfectly straight, arms crossed like the cadet commander liked to stand, but even McNair could hear the slight wobble in her voice.

"You can hit the bunk if you want to," McNair said. "It's probably the smart thing to do, use less air. I'm going to watch the villagers on the drone feeds." Not the live footage, or not just. She needed to know why the chief had destroyed Jarvis' leg like that. But she couldn't bring herself to say it. She didn't convey feelings of guilt correctly; people tended to think she was less than sympathetic. Better keep that to herself.

Resnick and Jarvis closed the semi-rigid curtains to their bunks. Jarvis' had been left open, but the drugs had fully kicked in, and she was sleeping the sleep of those no longer totally confined to reality.

McNair played the videos back over and over. There was probably no way she was ever going to understand their words, not before the rescue shuttle arrived. But could she figure out their intent?

Those two things were never quite the same, words and intent. McNair had always had an extensive vocabulary for her age from the moment she had learned to speak. She picked up technical speak and specialized lingo without ever having to hear a term more than once. And yet, also from a young age, she had learned that what people meant by the words they said seldom matched up to the dictionary definition. Every word was shaded with a meaning that wasn't quite the dictionary one, and a sentence was always larger than the sum of its parts. She couldn't just listen to the words and get anyone's meaning, she always had to be watching for all the other cues, the tip of the head that said "I'm just kidding," the raising of the eyebrows that said "I'm asking a question not making a statement," the twitch of just the very corner of the mouth that said "I'm being sarcastic." Getting the meaning meant finding the intent and that was exhausting work.

But it was work McNair had spent a lifetime toiling at. She could do this.

She played back the videos again, this time zipping through at double time. Then she doubled it again, and then again. Now the Sowmyathans' movements looked almost human. A bit herky-jerky but at least at an understandable speed.

And she caught it, the little gesture the chief had made when he had touched the rock-shuttle. He had pointed – barely more than a hint of movement she had missed in the moment – at first Smith and then Jarvis, and he had turned his palms over in a gesture that McNair was sure meant "I'm asking a question."

And McNair saw herself glance towards Jarvis. She didn't remember doing it in the moment, but she could see it now. He pointed to both of her fellow cadets, and she had indicated to him that Jarvis was the one.

The one who what?

She had shown the shuttle was trapped. He seemed to understand that.

Did he think she was a prisoner? Was he trying to help her get free by taking out her captor?

Certainly, they all seemed confused by how McNair and Smith responded to the chief's sudden attack. The world outside the shuttle had gone full dark before they had all gone back to their homes. It was hard to tell with their slow, plodding gait, but McNair thought it looked a little more downtrodden than usual. Perhaps end of the day tiredness, or perhaps, like she, they were burdened with a guilt they couldn't correctly express.

McNair slumped back in her chair, stewing, for what felt like hours.

Then she sat up, switched on her central monitor, and set to work. The workstation was mostly geared towards receiving and recording video feeds, but she had a program that would let her edit footage. Crudely, but it would be enough.

By dawn, she had assembled a collection of video fragments she hoped would tell their tale. Without waking the others, she suited up and headed out the airlock, over the ridge, and down the rocky hill to the village.

"I saw you, you know," a voice said in her head. Smith, awake and on comm.

"I think I can fix this," McNair said. "They didn't mean to hurt Jarvis. Well, they did, but they thought they were helping me. I think. But I can fix this."

"I trust you," Smith said. "What do you need from me?"

"Maybe just watch me, in case I run into trouble," McNair said.

"Cadet McNair, I've got your back."

McNair was glad she was alone, that the camera in her helmet faced out into the world and not back at her face, that no one could see how she flushed with pleasure to know that someone, anyone, but maybe especially Cadet Smith, had her back.

The Sowmyathans saw her coming and gathered in the open space between their houses to wait for her. She had seen the houses on the drone feeds where they had looked like they had been tunneled out of large boulders. Up close she could appreciate finer details, a carving that left fine grooves like brushwork at contrasting angles all over the surface, little repeating geometric shapes running around the openings that served as doors and windows. It might not be language, but it was definitely art. She had been right. No one could argue with what she was getting on video feed now.

She stopped in front of the chief and gave a little bow, mostly because she suddenly felt incredibly awkward. She was the very last person who should be attempting to communicate with others. The very last. And yet, maybe she was the only one who could.

Taking a deep breath, she touched the communications panel on the forearm of her suit and began the hologram display.

The villagers recoiled at the image suddenly appearing in their midst, a few of the younger ones even going suddenly liquid as the chief had the day before. But they quickly realized they were looking at themselves and drew closer, fascinated.

She didn't know the words, and she was sure what she was playing back would make as much sense as when they had played with the translation programs in linguistics class, changing from descendent language to descendent language and back to Galactic Union Standard and laughing at the strangeness that barely contained the original meaning. But hopefully, enough stayed true that they would understand what she was trying to tell them.

"No hard feelings," McNair whispered inside her helmet. "You wanted to help; you didn't understand. Jarvis is going to be OK."

"Do they understand you?" Smith asked.

"I don't know," McNair said. "I'm just hoping that they know we are trying. Trying should count."

"Now what are you showing them?" Smith asked. Holograms on a video feed tended to show up as grainy, jumpy images. She could see that something had changed, but she couldn't see exactly what.

"I'm trying to show them what we need," McNair said. "Help flagging down our shuttle. They must have a concept of being lost."

"I hope so," Smith said.

Then, one by one, the villagers started looking up into the sky. Then, in pairs, they began to confer. And, in family groups, they retreated back into their homes.

"Oh," Smith said when McNair found herself alone in the center of the square. "Oh, I'm sorry. That seemed to be going so well."

"It was a long shot," McNair said. But she felt that at least they had understood no one was mad about Jarvis. For McNair, that was the main thing. The rescue shuttle would find them sooner or later. Hopefully before Jarvis' pain meds ran out.

McNair lingered in the square for several minutes, but none of the villagers appeared to be coming back. She turned to trudge back up the hill to the shuttle. When she was halfway up the hill, she heard Smith gasp.

"What is it?"

"I don't know," Smith said. "Resnick's drones. They've been kind of wandering about since the villagers dispersed last night. Some of them caught something... hold on."

McNair did not take that to mean stand still. She jogged the rest of the way up the hill, cycled through the airlock, and barely took the time to toss her helmet aside before lunging to lurk over the back of Smith's chair. "What is it?"

"Look," Smith said, pointing to the screen. "The roofs of their houses. They just... light up."

"With what? They don't have a power source. Nothing we ever saw," McNair said.

"I don't know. Maybe luminescent bacteria, who knows? But look, they are signaling. Every one of them is pointing towards our shuttle."

"That's amazing," McNair said. They had understood her. They just hadn't grasped all the conversational niceties to convey that understanding to her. Having been given a mission, they had switched focus to fulfilling that mission, not reassuring her about anything.

"You don't know the half of it," Smith said, leaning back in her seat with her arms crossed and grinning up at McNair. "This image isn't even the village you were just talking to. This is villages all over this continent. Resnick's drones are all over the place, and they are seeing this everywhere. I think it's a safe bet that everywhere on the planet, the villages are pointing the way to us. You did good."

McNair never knew how to handle praise. She didn't want to come across as thinking too much of herself, but when she tried to brush it aside somehow the person giving her the compliment always took it as her condescending to them. She didn't know what she was doing wrong.

Instead, she changed the subject. "We should finish our report. They might go easier on us for breaking the rules if we at least got all our work done."

"They're going to go easy on us because of your brilliant breakthrough," Smith said but went to roust Resnick and Jarvis so we could gather again in a circle and go over the questions on the scouting report.

We had just finished up when the rescue shuttle arrived. Their whoops of delight turned somber when the pilot's voice came over the comm.

"Survey shuttle D7, is your airlock functioning?" he demanded.

"Yes sir," Smith replied.

"Then you will all proceed directly from your airlock to ours. There will be no deviations, not one step that isn't directly from there to here, is that understood?"

"Yes, sir. We do have a wounded crew member, sir," Smith said.

"Can she move?"

Smith looked to Jarvis who sat up higher in her bunk and gave a grim nod. "Yes, sir," Smith

"We have medics on board. Come over directly, and we'll tend to your crew member. I hope you cadets understand you're in a whole mess of trouble. One hurt crew member isn't going to soften the hearts of anyone at Planetary Exploration."

"The pilot and copilot-" Smith began.

"They were ejected from the cockpit at the moment of decompression by the emergency systems. We picked them up in space," the pilot said. "They were higher priority than you, but we knew right where you were. No need to light up the whole planet to point the way. We're good at our jobs, cadets."

"Yes, sir," Smith said almost meekly. She and Resnick helped Jarvis maneuver her injured leg into her pressure suit, and then the four of them left the crashed shuttle behind. McNair brought up the rear, Resnick and Smith both helping Jarvis limp over the rocky ground. As they were walking someone from the rescue shuttle passed them going the other way. Careful to keep every step directed towards the rescue shuttle, McNair turned her head to watch as the figure in the pressure suit climbed to the top of their wreck and placed something on the top of the craft. Then he jogged away from the crashed shuttle, passing the four of them once more.

They were nearly to the rescue shuttle's airlock when a flash of light reflecting off the windows in the airlock hatch had McNair looking back again. An incendiary device, to remove all traces of the shuttle that was never supposed to be on the surface. Nothing would be left but a smoking crater. Quite useless, McNair was certain. The entire planet already knew of its existence; there was no undoing that act.

They cycled through the airlock, and the medic waiting for them on the other side helped Jarvis to a seat and strapped her in before taking a look at her leg. This was a transport shuttle, not a scout shuttle, and had two long rows of seats down each side of the bulkhead with built-in storage bins down the center for stowing equipment. Resnick left an open seat between her and Jarvis, so the medic had room to work but reached across to take Jarvis' hand and hold it tight as the medic adjusted the cast.

McNair went all the way aft to the seat farthest from the others, but to her surprise Smith followed her, buckling herself in the very next seat. McNair didn't know if she was supposed to say something, but since Smith wasn't saying anything either she stayed silent.

She needed her bunk back on the space station. She needed to slide the door shut and decompress alone in her own quiet space for a few days.

She probably wasn't going to get that.

"Prepare for take-off," the pilot said over the intercom, still sounding tersely annoyed.

"We should have sat still and just waited," McNair said, the words out of her mouth before she realized she was more than just thinking them. Smith winced.

"I guess you're right. Still, we did something here. We broke the rules, but what we did, what you did, that's got to show potential. They have to see that." She didn't sound at all sure, and the more she tried to inject confidence into her voice the more doomed McNair was sure they all were.

Several hours later when the shuttle docked on the station, the medic got to her feet first and gathered up her gear. Resnick and Jarvis reached to unbuckle their belts.

"Just sit tight," the medic told them as she opened the airlock and set her bag inside. "Security will be escorting you to the briefing room as soon as I'm out."

"Security?" Resnick repeated, looking at Jarvis then at Smith.

"We broke the rules," McNair said.

"They're just trying to scare us," Resnick said.

"Mission accomplished," Smith muttered under her breath, too low for the others to hear. McNair looked at her hand on the armrest between them. She could hold it, like Resnick had done with Jarvis. But how hard did one squeeze, and for how long? She had no clue and kept her hands to herself.

"Cadets," a guard called from the now-open airlock. "Everyone out."

Resnick and Smith helped Jarvis limp out, and McNair followed. Only two guards were waiting for them, and they weren't waiting with cuffs or anything. That was something.

"Jarvis should report to medical?" Resnick asked.

"Negative. You're all going to be thoroughly debriefed first."

McNair felt her stomach drop. Debrief, that meant talking. Lots of talking. Lots of questions about what this or that thing you said really meant. She was going to fail at this, no question.

She felt someone clutch her hand and hold it, not tightly but not letting go either. Smith.

"We're in this together," she said to McNair. "We're going to get through this together."

Then she had to let McNair's hand go because cadets didn't walk down hallways holding hands. Not in uniform, anyway.

They had been briefed on the details of their scouting mission just days before, so the route the guards led them down was a familiar one, but rather than taking them to one of the large rooms with rows of desks circling the same projector they were put into separate impossibly tiny rooms. Resnick and Jarvis made little gasps of dismay, but McNair just walked inside the room the guard pointed her to and sat down on one side of the bare table, folded her hands on her lap, and waited.

And waited. And waited. She supposed the waiting was part of the punishment. Sometimes she thought she could hear the murmur of conversations around her, but that was impossible. Every mission briefing was considered classified to one level or another; all these rooms big and small were completely sound-proof. She was only imagining it. But still, she couldn't shake the certainty that everyone else was being talked to but her. Why else was she alone so long?

She had been the one to come up with the plan, after. It hadn't been her idea to go out of the ship, but communicating with the aliens, really making actual contact, that had all been on her. She should have kept her thoughts to herself.

Finally, there was a loud click, and the door swung open. Captain McGahan, McNair's commanding officer, step into the room, but McNair was surprised to see Lieutenant Rathers close on the captain's heels. There was only one chair, and the captain took it, setting his tablet on the table and running his fingers over the screen without looking up at McNair even once. McNair glanced up at Rathers leaning against the far wall with his arms crossed over his chest. McNair searched for any hint, any clue as to what her counselor was thinking, but came up with nothing.

The captain cleared his throat and pinned her with his steely eyes. "Start from the beginning and tell me everything that happened."

McNair told her entire version of events from beginning to end. Once she was done, the captain started with the questions. Every detail was scrutinized, and McNair fought waves of panic. She was so tired; her brain was a fog; she was sure was contradicting herself completely by accident. She looked to Lieutenant Rathers several times, but he never said a word, just watched her as she struggled to answer and explain her answers and clarify her explanations.

At one point there was a knock at the door, and a cadet came in to whisper something in the captain's ear. He stared at McNair the entire time he listened, his eyes boring into her, and she looked down at her own hands.

She was never getting that assignment now.

The captain said something to the cadet, too low for McNair to hear, and the door shut once more.

"I believe we covered everything?" the captain said, turning to look at Lieutenant Rathers.

"Yes, sir," the lieutenant said.

"OK, I'm sealing the audio record now," the captain said, touching his tablet. "Cadet McNair, once you're done here, you're to hit your bunk. You'll be standing before the disciplinary committee at 0600, full dress uniform. I expect to find you rested and prepared to receive your verdict." He stood up but paused halfway to the door.

"And do something with your hair. I know you were in a shuttle crash, but you're still in uniform, cadet. Make an effort."

"Yes, sir," McNair said, running her hands over her head to smooth the mess back. She doubted it did much good.

Rathers slid into the chair across from her and finally looked at her.

"An interesting first assignment," he said.

"I know I messed up," McNair said.

"Did you? It seemed to be a rousing success to me."

McNair looked up at him sharply. Was he joking? He had to be joking. But why would he mess with her like that, now?

"Your team messed up, no doubt about that," Rathers said. "And you'll be facing that music in the morning. But you're a part of the team now. You succeeded at that."

"What do you mean?"

"Your fellow cadets all speak very highly of you. And they all repeatedly pointed out that you had been the sole dissenting vote in making first contact. They were very clear on that point. But in your version of events, you never mention that at all. You just reported it as the outcome of a vote."

"That's what it was," McNair said. "A vote. I lost. I wasn't persuasive enough."

"I think you have more pull with them now than before," Rathers said. "This is off the record, I'm just curious, but why didn't you mention you had voted against to the captain? Perhaps save yourself a little punishment?"

"We took a vote as a team. The team acted. And we should face the consequences as a team. Right?" she asked, uncertain.

"I can think of lots of exceptions to that," Rathers said, "including possibly this one. You four made a big mistake."

McNair looked down at her folded hands and bit her lip hard enough to taste blood.

"But," Rathers said. "Planetary Exploration is having trouble working out just what you did, your communications breakthrough. I expect the four of you will be on station duty for the next rotation at least, consulting with them. And you're going to have to really impress to ever see another scout mission or any another kind of off-station duty."

"But will still be working together?"

Rathers sat back with a smile. "The captain intended to break the four of you up into separate details, but then you gave your version of events where the other three were crucial to your breakthrough, and, well…"

"But they were," McNair said. "Resnick's drones, Smith's guidance, Jarvis' leg."

"Hey, I'm glad you get to stick with people you're comfortable with. You have talents that are going to serve the Galactic Union very well, but you have some defects to be corrected too. That work might never end. You're going to need some support to do it. I know I'm not enough. But hopefully, now that you have a team that works together in a bigger than the sum of its parts kind of way, you can use that for better ends next time."

"Yes, sir," McNair said.

After too short a sleep she got into her dress uniform and went to the lavatory to wet comb her hair into some semblance of order. The other three were already there, each in front of a different mirror, patting their hair into place. The leg of her uniform bulged over the cast, and she was leaning on two crutches, but her face was looking much less tight and gray. They all turned to look at her when she came in, and she almost flinched from so many eyes on her at once.

"McNair," Smith said. "Come here. Let us do something with your hair."

"My hair?" she all but squeaked.

"Yes," Resnick said. "You should look more like you're one of us."

"Erm," McNair said. She didn't want to admit that she had seen how much time those victory rolls took to do up, and she was never going to spend that much time on such a pointless pursuit.

"Not exactly like us," Smith said, still regarding her much too closely. McNair fought the urge to squirm. "No, you want a different look. Something a little softer here, but tidier here." Her fingers were dancing all around McNair's head, not quite touching her. McNair couldn't see what she was talking about, but Resnick was nodding her approval.

"And the color," Resnick said. "That definitely needs to go. Not now, obviously, but soon."

"Definitely lose the color," Jarvis agreed.

Smith stepped back to consider her. "I'm thinking something… black. Shiny black. Like those creatures."

"Or like deep space?" McNair offered.

"Like deep space," Smith agreed with a smile that McNair felt was 100% genuine. And she even managed to smile back. It didn't really matter if they got punished or pushed back a year or any of it. Someday she'd get that posting she wanted, and when that day came, she would know that somewhere else in the vastness of the universe three women happily had her back.

UPON THE LONESOME WILD

The house is too quiet at night these days. Instead of the sounds of my children breathing, snoring, stirring restlessly in their beds I hear things moving through the fields outside. Slow sinuous things stirring the leaves on the tall stalks, larger rushing things that shake the ears of corn and great tromping things that snap the stalks themselves.

I stop telling my husband what I hear in the night. He still insists the only living things on this planet are what we brought with us. Rats tagged along, they always do, he said, but what I'm hearing is not rats.

And the soft whispering movements that I have to strain to hear are more frightening than the stomping destruction. They get closer to our little house, every night a little closer.

Most mornings I wake far too early, before the sun has even risen. My husband is already up and gone, tinkering in his shed until there is enough light to start working in the fields. My days have too much time to fill with too little to do, so I lie in bed, looking out the curved glass that is both wall and ceiling, a remnant of when our house was also a greenhouse and we lived and slept among the young plants too delicate yet for the foreign landscape. I watch as the grays of the world outside transition to more familiar greens and blues, but once the sun winks over the horizon straight into my sleepy eyes I get up and shuffle down to the kitchen.

I fill my kettle from the water recycler and switch it on then spoon tea into the basket of my teapot. The tin is nearly empty and there's only one other in the pantry to last me the rest of my life, but I don't skimp. No more ships from Earth means no more tea but I'd rather savor these last days of full-strength tea every day with breakfast than try to stretch it out and make it last. I might regret that later, but I doubt it. This way my memories will always be of proper tea, not sporadic cups of weak, watery, unsatisfying tea.

I'm just finishing my toast with soft-cooked egg when I hear our transport setting down in front of my house. I assumed my husband was in the shed, but he was in town. I meet him at the door.

"Any news?" I ask. He shakes his head, but there is a twinkle in his eye.

"I have something for you," he says and unzips his field coat. Suddenly I have a warm, trembling, white-haired thing in my arms.

"Lou!" I cry. "A dog!"

"Still a puppy," Lou says. "Mal found it near the shuttle port. Someone who left on the last ship must have left this little fellow behind."

"What's this?" My fingers run over a bald patch in the dog's fur, a smooth burn scar.

"Mal reckons he was mistreated before he was abandoned. He bites. A lot. Mal can't handle him on his own but I said you could use a challenge."

"I didn't know anyone had decanted a dog," I say as I carry the dog into the kitchen and fill a bowl with water. Once upon a time we had talked of a dog of our own, but it was going to come after chickens, goats, and sheep. We never got past chickens.

"The southern farms had rodent troubles. They decanted cats mostly but a few breeds of dogs like this one. He's a rat terrier."

"A working dog," I say.

"Once you train him up a bit," Lou says. "Mal tells me just one of these guys can take out dozens of rats a day. That should help you sleep at night."

I smile and kiss his cheek. I'm grateful for the company, and having a dog to care for and train will indeed go a long way towards filling my days with activity. But what is keeping me awake at night is definitely not rats.

Lou refuels from the coffee dispenser that is always full of fresh, hot coffee - we're decades away from running out of that - then heads out to all of the multitude of tasks that await a farmer. He doesn't let the fact that no more ships will be coming to take what we harvest slow him down. Even when I can see the weariness of the years of labor weighing on his shoulders I do not suggest he rest more. If he starts to make time to rest, he'll just start dwelling on how useless it all turned out to be. It will kill him.

After a little research and much careful consideration I name my puppy Heimdallr. In addition to hunting rats he's bred to be a watchdog, sounding the alarm at any sign of danger, and while I have yet to see him hunt he does bark, almost constantly. He's a lot more work than any of my babies were, so anxious, hyper, biting at my ankles as I walk, always trying to stop me moving about. I research dog training and work diligently to change his behavior, work even more diligently not to lose my own temper when his sharp puppy teeth cut my skin again and again. But change he does. He doesn't get any calmer, more redirecting his biting energy into sprinting through the fields or jumping into the air. The little fellow can jump so high our eyes are on a level at his apex. The biting doesn't stop completely, it's more like when he is overwhelmed with doggy emotion he closes his mouth over my wrist and looks at me, his brown eyes arguing that he isn't biting per se, just hugging me with his mouth. Then he lets go and gently licks my skin. It's hard to be mad with him.

I make a little bed for him in our bedroom but when Lou gets up in the gray before dawn Heimdallr watches him go then rushes to jump onto the bed and curl against my belly, catching the sleeves of my nightshirt in his teeth and adjusting my arms to wrap around him. I scratch all around his ears as we wait for the world to brighten.

Sometimes his ears perk up, his muscles stiffening as if he uses his whole body to listen. Then I hear it too, the rustling through the leaves. He growls so low it's nearly subsonic, as if he doesn't want to drown out the sound of whatever it is approaching. I try to soothe him - even sequestered in his shed Lou finds the sound of the dog barking irritating - but he remains at quivering high alert until the rustling fades away. Then he flops back down against me but sits with his head up, resolute not to sleep while danger remains hidden somewhere in those fields.

In the morning our closest neighbor Flo stops by. This is unusual; she and her husband Steve have always shared all their work equally so even though their children have also gone she is still busy working the fields.

"They're in the corn," she says. I'm startled and nearly slosh as I'm pouring out the tea.

"They?"

"Rats," Flo says and scrunches up her nose. I feel a sharp ache as the hope that I would have someone to talk to about what I hear in the night flames out. Heimdallr nudges my knee with my nose. He knows I'm not crazy.

"Lou said they had those in the southern farms," I say at last.

"Well, they're moving north. There is a band of feral cats that follows them, but the numbers are against them."

"The dog here is supposed to be good with rats," I say.

"Too late for us," Flo says. "We're packing up."

"Leaving? Is another ship coming?"

"No, we're just moving into the shuttle port. Some of the others are already there. Tearing down the interior walls, remodeling the space. It will be a nice community, all of us together like when we were kids."

"That sounds lovely," I smile. It had been a lovely childhood, back on the ship.

"You could come too," Flo says.

"Oh, no," I say. "Lou."

"That's what I thought you'd say, but I had to ask," Flo says. She doesn't tease me about Lou's loner ways. She used to every time we got together, but not now. I appreciate her silence.

Flo and I finish our tea as well as the lemon bread she had brought with her, then she kisses my cheek and promises to say good-bye before they head into town. I haven't been to town since my youngest got on his shuttle. She doesn't mention that either.

I clean up the few dishes and am just heading outside with Heimdallr for our morning walk when the computer chimes an incoming message. These come more and more rarely as my children move away from me at approaching relativistic speeds. Heimdallr hears or scents something and runs past me out the door to plunge into the stalks of corn that surround our home. I let him go, turning back into the kitchen to touch the nearest console. The message is from my eldest, the first to leave nearly twelve years ago, but not looking a day older than when he left. He sends us chatty messages about his duties on the ship. He won't live to see his ship's destination, will likely not even be drawn in the lottery to produce offspring to replace the crew. All of my other children away on other ships heading to other potential colony planets face the same future.

It's just as well I'm watching this without Lou at my side. He was the last born on our own ship to replace an aging crew member. The last child born before him was ten already, too old for companionship, and Lou himself was ten before my generation, the first of the colonizing children, were born. So many of us, twenty a year for sixteen years before we reached this planet, our great hope. Lou was raised to expect the exact life my children are leading, working to some future you aren't likely to see, a minimal number of people around you keeping the ship going. A quiet, nearly solitary life.

But I was raised to be one of a crowd of workers, part of a community. I'm not sure what drew Lou to me. He once said I seemed the quietest of a very noisy pack of girls. Me, I was flattered that someone so mature chose me. We got along well enough, but there were challenges. Lou couldn't stand the chaos of children our house soon became and spent more and more time on his own in the fields or in his shed, coming in long after bedtime, heading out in the earliest of hours. For my part, six children were far too few, but when it became clear that the planet that had passed all preliminary tests for colonization was simply not able to support our agricultural efforts, we had to stop having children.

And all of my children had to leave; it was that or remain with their aging parents on a dying planet. Every year the harvest is poorer than the year before, the corn blighted by causes that perhaps the brightest minds on Earth could work to discover but it's more cost-effective to write this world off and move on. We invested our lives in this colony, but back on Earth they only invested money.

I lived my life expecting a dozen children, a dozen-dozen grand-children clamoring around me in my last days. Instead I have a largely silent husband, and now a dog.

I leave the message light flashing so Lou will see it when he comes in for more coffee and head out to find where the dog has gone off to. As the door shuts behind me Heimdallr comes trotting out of the corn. Something is dangling from his mouth, something with a long whip-like tail and toes curled tight in the last throes of life. He sits down at my feet with the thing in his mouth but refuses to part with it. I go back into the house and find a bit of vat-beef and he reluctantly agrees to the exchange.

A rat.

I go into the part of our house that still serves as a greenhouse, where I keep herbs and a few fresh vegetables that still thrive, potted as they are in Earth soil. I find a trowel and go back outside to scoop up the remains and dump them into the biological recycler behind the shed. It will be fertilizer now. I stretch my back and look to the south. Hill after hill of abandoned fields, consumed by hungry rats now moving north.

It doesn't really matter, losing the crop. We have stores enough of food from Earth to feed us both for the rest of our days. But Lou will be broken. I don't want to tell him, but I don't want to keep it from him either.

Heimdallr gives a happy little bark and plunges back into the corn, tail wagging excitedly as he pursues another rat. I watch him go then push my way into the shed.

I'm momentarily startled to find my always-moving husband sitting in a chair, but quickly realize that even with his chin resting against his chest he's not napping.

I sit in the chair beside his, his hand in my lap, not stirring until at last Heimdallr finds me. He drops another rat at our feet then gently touches Lou's knee with his nose. He sits then lays down on the floor, nose between his paws but eyes on mine.

"Yes, you're right," I say to him and push myself to my feet. I pick up my trowel and bring the rat to the recycler. There are a few others at the edge of the corn and I collect those as well.

Lou is going to be harder.

My knees click as I walk back to the house and there is a dull ache in my low back. Those things are always there, but it s as if without seeing Lou, tired and always hurting somewhere, without having him to compare myself to I'm now feeling everything, the to l every year on this planet has taken on me.

Mal doesn't answer my call but I know Mal and leave him a brief message. He'll come running as soon as he gets it, but he can beat Lou with prolonged bouts of busy. I sit in the kitchen feeding Heimdallr bits of vat beef, not really hungry myself. When the beef is gone I take a tea towel down from its rung near the kettle and blot away the little salty liquid circles that had formed on the tabletop then turn out the lights and head upstairs to the bedroom. Heimdallr looks at his little bed but when I sit down on my own bed he jumps to join me, to curl up against my belly and pull my arms around him.

I never quite fall asleep; the silence is too deafening. It is nearly dawn before the corn begins to stir and Heimdallr wakes and growls.

"We don't know that it's dangerous, whatever it is," I say as he snuggles close. "It could be nothing. You like to bark a nothing, don't you?"

Heimdallr ignores this. We both know it's not nothing. But the idea that it's not dangerous is a new thought for me. Heimdallr continues to growl as the rustling grows nearer. I can see leaves on the stalks nodding and waving, right up to the very edge of the field. Heimdallr's growl becomes a bark, loud and shrill enough to make my old ears ring. At last he stops and comes back to my side. It takes a long time for my ears to adjust to the quiet, but I can see that the corn is still. Whatever had been approaching has turned back.

In the morning we go outside to investigate, but the corn looks like it always does. Heimdallr is initially skittish but forgets his nervousness at the first sign of a rat scurrying through the stalks. I take a chair out of the kitchen and set it in the yard facing the corn. The day passes around me, the sun climbing the sky, hovering there for a lazy lunchtime I don't indulge in then slowly falling towards the west. I sit and watch the sky darken as the sun sets behind me. Steve and Flo over the hill are burning something; the sky is tinged a smoky red and I can smell the headachy smell of something burned too green.

There is a sizeable pile of rats beside my chair when Mal at last arrives.

"Enid," he says in greeting. I want to get up from my chair, but I can't make myself do it, just nod. Heimdallr comes crashing out of the corn to jump all over Mal. Mal gets him settled down enough to be petted.

"He's in the shed?" Mal guesses. I nod. He turns and looks from the shed door to the recycler a short walk away then back at my chair.

"Why don't you head inside, get something to eat. Or better," he pats his pockets then pulls out a little flask, the metal warm on the side that had been pressed close to his thigh. "Have a splash of this. I'll be just a moment."

I nod again and push my way into the kitchen. Heimdallr runs past me to his water bowl and drinks it dry. I refill it and he drinks two more gulps then is finally sated. Hunting rats is thirsty work, apparently.

I look at the flask in my hand then set it on the kitchen table without opening it. Instead I make myself an unscheduled cup of tea. I hear the door on the recycler bang close and fill a mug with coffee from the dispenser, setting it on the table across from my tea. Then I power down the coffee maker that has been running continuously for more than thirty years. It was the first thing we turned on when the house was complete, even before the temperature controls.

Heimdallr gets back to his feet as Mal comes into the kitchen and washes his hands at the sink. He opens the flask, pouring the minutest of amounts into his coffee before taking a deep swallow.

"Something is burning," I say, because I can't talk about anything else.

"That's Steve and Flo," Mal says. "The rats took most of their crop. They're hoping a burn will be good for the soil." He gives a shrug and takes another swallow of coffee. I look at my tea, still untasted. He shifts in his chair, searching for more words. "Lou was a good man. A good farmer. More's the pity none of us ever got a chance to prove that."

"Yes," I say. "Well."

I walk him back to his transport, Heimdallr charging back into the corn the minute we're out the door.

"Are you going to be all right out here?"

"No reason not to be."

Mal nods but looks unconvinced. I watch the dust cloud that obscures his transport until it disappears over the hill to the south then sit back down in the chair facing the corn.

My house's shadow lengthens around me, reaching further and further out into the corn until it loses all definition and there is nothing but darkness. Heimdallr finds a few more rats but as the stars come out he lingers closer to me, occasionally running along the edge of the field, nose close to the ground, but not plunging back in among the stalks.

He killed dozens of rats today, but what I've heard in the corn isn't rats. Now it's too late to prove that to Lou, but I can prove it to myself.

Heimdallr settles at my side, occasionally snuffling at my hand, curious why we aren't going inside. I wait. The cold settles into my bones and my joints ache, but still I wait. When the wind shifts I can smell the remains of Steve and Flo's fields. They had driven the rats further north, to our fields. That's why Heimdallr is suddenly finding rats everywhere.

What about the other thing, the thing that slinks through the leaves at night? Did they live in Steve and Flo's fields as well as our own? Had they been driven north as well? Or are they unique to our farm? Ours the farthest north, the closest to the shallow river and the purplish moors beyond?

I doze in my chair, uncomfortable as it is, and the stars move across the sky in their habitual slow dance.

I'm on my feet before I even quite hear the rustling. Heimdallr is too, his hair on end and every muscle so tight he quivers. I want to step closer to the corn but I'm frozen in place, unable to do more than listen as the whispering rustle ripples through the leaves of corn. There is no wind. Heimdallr gives his low growl but stays close to my side.

I can see the corn moving, the stalks quivering, closer and closer. I lean forward, peering into the darkness. My night vision is as sharp as ever, but I've grown nearsighted and can't make out details at such a distance.

I take a step forward and blow out a breath as if that small step has been a tremendous effort. Heimdallr barks at me, a shrill, panicked bark. I take another step, easier this time. I can almost see... but not quite. I only see the leaves shaking, the stalks oh so gently displaced, but to make room for what? I take another step.

Heimdallr barks and jumps but I pay him no mind. I am at the edge of the corn now, my hands pushing into the green mass, parting leaves and stalks and shriveled ears. Heimdallr gives a low whine then lunges at me. His mouth closes on my ankle and I feel his teeth, less sharp now that his puppy teeth have fallen away to make room for adult teeth. He squeezes gently, carefully, but persistently.

The rustling is so close. I feel the leaves brushing against my outthrust fingertips. So close. I lean in.

Heimdallr's mouth squeezes harder, still not breaking the skin but trapping my ankle. He whines, and the sound breaks my heart. It breaks the world around me, or at least it breaks the spell, for I'm suddenly aware of myself, an old woman letting her imagination run away with her in the dark of night.

What was I doing?

The rustling stops as if my questioning has ceased its existence. I let my arms fall to my sides but remain at the edge of the fields, the fields that had slowly drained every bit of life out of my husband. Soon the husk that remains will be fertilizer and even that will be given to the corn. The droopy, useless corn no one is ever going to buy.

Heimdallr sits beside me, sniffing the air. He senses something I don't and barks, a questioning sort of bark.

The corn answers. I fall back, startled. Heimdallr for once is not the frightened one. He barks again, a happy bark of greeting. A cascade of happy barks responds to him and he wags his tail crazily.

Flo said there is a pack of cats that follows the rats. Perhaps there are other rat terriers as well? But then why don't they come out of the fields, into the starlight? Why doesn't Heimdallr go in to see them?

Heimdallr barks again then turns and runs back to the house, scratching at the door until I rouse myself to follow and let him in. My tea from the night before still sits untouched on the kitchen table but I walk on, all the way to my bedroom.

Heimdallr is the first on the bed this time and I curl myself around him, letting him rest his head in one cupped palm. He's not a cat but he seems so pleased with himself he's practically purring. The things in the corn, they want him to come to them, but he needs to be with me. He's not the fearful, biting, panicked creature he was the day we met, and the process of changing that changed us both. Partly it's that bond and the loyalty of a dog, but partly he's still afraid. He isn't ready to go into the corn without me, and I'm not sure I'm exactly welcome there.

I sleep until long after sunup. When I head back downstairs the tea is still waiting and although it's a travesty to do so I reheat it for my breakfast. Heimdallr's ears perk up at the sound of a transport setting down in the yard and we go outside to see Steve and Flo emerge from a transport loaded down with what looks like everything they own.

"Enid," Flo says and rushes to hug me. "Mal told us."

"I figured," I say.

"You should come with us," Flo says.

"Oh, I don't think so," I say.

"Enid," Flo says, in that lecturing voice I remember so well from our school days back on the generation ship. "Why stay out here all alone?"

"I'm not alone," I say and as I look out towards the corn Heimdallr looks back towards us, ears pulled high as if he senses we're talking about him.

"The dog is welcome too," Steve says. "Lots of us have cats already."

"Thank you for thinking of me, but I'm happy where I am," I say. "And I'm really not alone out here."

"There's Mal," Steve says and Flo concedes with a reluctant nod. I say nothing.

There is something out in that corn. Something that was here before us and will be here after we've all gone. Heimdallr isn't ready to meet it yet, but someday he will be. I can wait.

"Can we do anything for you?" Flo asks, hands gesturing helplessly.

Soon we'll all be gone, even the community in the shuttle port is only making themselves comfortable until the end comes. Soon there will be no trace of us, and life here will return to whatever it was before we ever came. Except for the rats. Whatever hides in the corn wants the rats gone, I'm sure of it. Perhaps they have already befriended the cats. Now they are befriending Heimdallr. They need Heimdallr to hunt rats, and Heimdallr needs me. For the rest of his life, he'll need me. That will be the rest of my life too.

It's a comfort, knowing the task that will fill the days before me.

Flo is still looking at me, worry etched deep around her eyes. What did she ask me? If I need anything? Do I?

"Actually," I say, "if you can find any tea. More tea would be lovely."

TEAR OF A SPHINX

The patter of the drums faded away and my mother's little footsteps slowed with it, leaving nothing but the eerie drone of the pipe and the long sweeping motions of my mother's arms, her entire body. I knew she was thinking of her home beyond the horizon where the wind made the sea of grass dance in the same lazy way.

And for a moment, just for an instant, I saw a shine in the sphinx's eye. I wasn't the only one who saw it; a wave of emotion rustled the crowd around me. We were all about to hold our breath, as if such a gesture could grant a wish or avert a fate.

But the moment was gone before a single one of us could suck in a breath to hold. My mother's arms wrapped to one side in preparation for a turn, the drummer's fingers hovering over the drum skin, about to tap out a dizzying beat. Then in a whisper of wind my mother lay broken under the sphinx's lion paw. No one screamed, not even my mother; the crunch of her spine echoed through the square before the palace like the crashes in the chariot races used to. Then the sphinx left her - broken but still alive, her blood draining away into the thirsty sand - to feast on the musicians.

Still no one screamed. We had seen this so many times since the sphinx had flown in from the east and planted herself on top of the palace. Screams were no help. Neither were tears, but those were harder to swallow down.

The crowd dispersed, not wanting to witness the sphinx at her meal. I crossed the shining sand to my mother's side and knelt beside her to take her hand. Her eyes were imploring and her lips worked to speak but all that came forth was a bubbly stream of spittle and blood. Then she was gone and I was alone.

———

I stand tall, arms high, muscles loose as I wave them back and forth, my body swaying I swear just like my mother's.

I see in her eyes she doesn't agree. Her arms drop, her teeth worrying her lip as she thinks.

"If I could just see the grass," I say, but she shakes her head. I know it is forbidden for us to leave the city, but that is not what she is thinking.

"Come, Sacmis," she says, taking my hand. We leave our master's house and cross the open square to the palace itself. My mother often gives lessons to the wives and daughters of the king and is always welcome in the queens' rooms and gardens. It is the hottest part of the day and the ladies of the court are napping on benches or on blankets spread under trees as my mother brings me to a courtyard beyond the great fountain. Against the wall is a large oval of polished bronze.

My mother has a mirror, a little circle no bigger than the palm of her hand, a rare treasure I occasionally am allowed to play with. The queens' mirror is so large I can see my entire body in it, and my mother's as well as she stands beside me.

She lifts her arms and begins to sway and I follow. Again I am certain my moves are exactly like hers, but the mirror shows me they are not. I reach higher, sway looser, but I only look more awkward the harder I try.

I stop.

"I'm not like grass," I say, running my hands down my thick arms, shaking the feet at the ends of my rounded legs. Someday I may be as tall as my mother but I will never be wispy.

"But you love to dance," my mother says, and I nod. "We just have to find your dance."

———

I was still holding my mother's hand when the sun sank into its resting place between the two mountains to the west and the evening birds began their chatter. I heard footsteps and lifted my head to see the priests approaching. The sphinx was watching them too, but her eyelids were heavy, each blink seeming like it would be the last, but sleep never took her. Many dead warriors could attest to that fact.

The priests worked quickly but silently, gathering up the remains of the musicians and carrying them back to the temple. The high priest came to my side, laying a hand on my shoulder.

"She was not eaten, let that be a comfort to you. Now she will have her body whole and intact for the journey to the underworld. Surely she will dance in the halls of the king of the dead."

I nodded, not comforted.

"You should return home now. Your family must be looking for you."

"I have no home without her," I said, still squeezing her hand tight. "I want to stay with her."

"We must start the embalming process at once," the priest said. "It is forbidden for any but priests to witness these rites. But if you wish you may stay in the temple until the rites are completed, to be near your mother."

"Thank you," I said, reluctantly letting go of my mother's hand as two of the younger acolytes came to take her away. The high priest put an arm around me to lead me away.

I felt a tickle up my spine and looked back. The sphinx's eyes were slipping shut once more, but I knew she had been watching me. Balefully.

———

My mother laughs as the dance master praises her exotic style.

"It is just a country dance among my people," she says. "All the girls do it, many better than I."

I shift my weight from foot to foot, feeling my failure more acutely.

"Your dances of fire and sand take incredible skill to master, " my mother goes on, and the master acknowledges this with a pleased nod. "I would like my daughter to study with you."

The master turns to me as if just noticing me there. He frowns.

"We usually start the training much younger."

"She is only eight, and she is a fast learner. She has been dancing with me since birth. In truth, before."

The master gives a little laugh. My mother is known throughout the city, and the tale of how her dancing stole the heart of the merchant Panhsj is famous. The journey to find the father of her unborn child ended that day; it no longer mattered.

"I will take her on as my own special student," the master says.

————

My mother's body was carried into the temple and down to the chambers where I could not follow. I remained before the statue of the death god.

Among my mother's people the dead were put into the earth, buried curled up like babies in the womb, decked in flowers and with their most personal possessions with them, but in all aspects it was a simple ceremony, quickly over and done. I wondered if she would prefer it to what was about to happen, the long embalming process then the journey down the river to be placed in the city of the dead in the building Panhsj had bought for his family when he had made this city at the center of the world his home.

She would want whatever made Panhsj happy, and he would follow the ways of his adopted people.

The temple was quiet, the soft hiss of the burning oil lamps only occasionally popping as a moth drew too close and met its end. I went back outside onto the steps overlooking the square. The moon was rising behind the palace, outlining the form of the sphinx where she roosted on the king's patio. So much had changed since she had flown in during the celebration of the young prince's marriage. She had killed hundreds that first day.

I went back inside, to get away from the eyes that always seemed to be turned my way. In the anteroom was Panhsj asking a servant with an armful of wood if he had seen me.

"Here I am, " I called.

"Thank the gods you are unhurt," he said. "When no one could find you I didn't know what to think."

"I'm a slave, it's forbidden for me to leave the city," I said. "Of course I'm still here."

"Why do you say such things? No one has ever treated you as a slave. I loved you mother with all my heart, and you have always been as a daughter to me."

I said nothing, just twisted the iron bangle on my wrist.

"You wish to leave the city?" he asked.

"I don't wish to stay here to watch everyone get eaten one by one by that cursed monster."

"She will be appeased, all the auguries tell us so."

"Mother almost succeeded," I said.

"I know," Panhsj said, wiping away a tear, one tear more than the sphinx had shed.

"Who can succeed where she failed?"

"The augurs are searching for that answer," he said, but he sounded no more hopeful than I.

"I wish to stay here with my mother until she makes her final journey," I said.

"Of course," he said, too briskly. "Then?"

"I don't know."

"We'll talk again when the time comes," he said. "Try to rest. It will be days before your mother will be ready to go up the river. Are you sure you don't want to come home?"

"Yes, I'm sure. I need to be here now."

"Then that is where you shall be."

He gave me a kiss on the forehead and departed.

———

"I do not have the body for sand or fire dancing anymore than I do for the grass dance," I say. Sand dancing requires high leaps my stouter form can't manage and fire dancing like the dance of grass wants long, sinewy arms to make the intricate hand movement look artful. My pudgy hands make it all look so awkward.

"You're not done growing yet," my mother says as she continues braiding my hair. "Someday you will be taller even than I." Mother is a head taller than the women in the city, taller even than many of the men.

"Wider, too," I say.

"Your father was the biggest man I've ever seen," she says. "His shoulders were immense. His arms were thicker than most men's thighs."

"I don't want to be a hulking giant," I say.

"Your father was a hunter, He moved like a cat, slow and silent but always ready to pounce. You will grow into your body. You will learn how to move inside of it."

"I should train with hunters maybe," I say.

"But you love to dance."

I say nothing. I am beginning to fear that love may not be enough.

———

I was dreaming of the sphinx, of her eyes watching me even through the walls of the temple. Why did I feel like she was watching me, specifically now? Even if she had shared a moment with my mother, had come close to shedding that one necessary tear as my mother used all of her art to dance her dance of homesickness for the sea of grass, surely she had no such connection with me. I looked so little like my mother, danced like her even less.

Still the eyes haunted me until a firm hand shook me awake. I shed confusion and disorientation like layers of bedclothes, finally sitting up to find myself on the floor of the temple with Panhsj's son Aapep kneeling beside me.

"Aapep," I said and fell into his arms. We had been born on the same day, the very day my mother had entered the city as Panhsj's slave purchased on his way home from trading with his homeland. He had always been like a brother to me.

"She's gone," I said.

"I know. I saw."

Of course he had seen. He had been standing beside me as we watched my mother dance. I had lost him in the chaos when the violence started, or he had lost me.

"You should come home, eat something, sleep in your own bed," Aapep said when my tears had quieted down.

"I wish to stay here, near her. Until she goes."

"That won't be possible," Aapep said. There was something in his voice, a bitter pain he struggled to hide from me. I sat back, looking at him with all the hard intensity of the sphinx herself.

"What happened?"

"The augurs have said you must try next."

"That's impossible."

"They have foreseen."

"Nothing else they have foreseen has come to pass. How many singers, painters, poets, artists have tried to move that stone heart to part with a single tear? All dead now, every one of them. If my mother could not do it, what chance have I?"

"Better than the rest of us, or so the augurs say."

"And because I am a slave I have no say."

"Your mother was also a slave, but she was not forced. She asked to have her turn same as all free people of this city."

"It meant nothing. She failed and she is gone."

"You will succeed. It is foreseen."

"I see in your eyes you don't believe it either."

Aapep looked away, up at the death god towering over us.

"Do you want to flee? I will help you. If that's what you want I will get you past the gates. But I don't know where you could go."

"To my mother's people. Or further, to my father's people."

"You've never felt like we are your people?"

I managed a weak smile. "*You* are my people, Aapep. You will always be my brother. But this city is not the place for me."

"Your mother made her home here. Even as a slave she had fame as a dancer, and you know the money she earned was her own. My father never took a thing from her or forbid her any wish."

"Save leaving."

"Those are the laws of the city. And, Sacmis, I do not believe leaving was ever her wish."

"Nor I," I admitted. There was a rustle of sandals on the stone floor and Panhsj had returned with the augurs and the grand vizier.

"I will do it," I said before any of them could say a word. "In exchange for this," I said, raising my wrist with its tight iron bangle.

"So be it," the grand vizier said with a bow.

I was taken to the palace and fed whatever I asked for from the king's own kitchens. The king himself came to thank me for what I was about to do, but I saw no hope in his eyes. No one believed this was more than just another in a long line of attempts to appease the sphinx.

Then I was brought to a bedchamber and left alone to sleep.

As if I could.

After the sphinx slaughtered the royal wedding guests and roosted atop the palace the people of the city spent a long time not knowing what she wanted. She just watched us as we scurried through the streets, not daring to be out in the open for longer than necessary. Occasionally some random person would catch her attention and she would swoop down, tearing their bodies apart with her lion claws, striking their faces with her snake-headed tail. Some she ate, more she merely destroyed and left bleeding into the dry sand.

Her roost overlooking the city square made it impossible to set up the market. A few merchants tried to start a small market on the outskirts of the city; that had ended in dozens more dead.

Then the augurs had divined that the sphinx watched us because she wanted to find the essence of human experience. Once she had learned that, she would leave. Then old scrolls were found deep in the archives, history of a previous sphinx who had been moved by one young boy's voice raised in song to shed a single tear then depart.

At first there was bitter competition for the honor of performing for the sphinx, but soon the number of artists began to dwindle. Some she would observe until their performance was done, others she barely let get started, but all ended up mangled in the sand or eaten.

The lesser artists began to disappear, fleeing the city in the dark of night. Itinerant performers came, drawn by tales of the sphinx and the hope of instant fame and the gratitude of a king. But not many.

Then the warriors and hunters took their turn. Alone, in groups, with strange war machines or with clever traps, they all failed and died horribly.

The sphinx was unmoved.

When tributes came before the sphinx she would content herself with only killing those, but when there were no volunteers she would grow restless and strike at whomever she found.

One day she landed in the queens' gardens and hunted down and mutilated every queen, princess, lady-in-waiting and servant she could find. Many of them had been my mother's friends, students she had trained from early childhood to adulthood.

She wept. We all wept. The sphinx was destroying everything of beauty in the city.

Then my mother asked to perform, and Panhsj wept.

"I can refuse you nothing, but please don't ask this," he said.

"I think I can succeed," my mother said. "I think I understand her heart."

"Such a monster has no heart," Panhsj's wife said.

"I think she longs for a home she can never return to," my mother went on. "I am happy here, but still I know that longing. I can do this."

The discussion went through the night, but my mother got her wish.

The sphinx was unmoved.

———

In the morning I bathed and selected an outfit from the heaps of clothes left behind by the massacred royal women.

I didn't know what I could do. None of my dances were good enough. My mother was the best, but she had failed. Better sand dancers and fire dancers than I had failed. What could I possibly do?

A servant came into the room, bowing. "I was sent to inquire what musicians you will require? There are few left, and none of real quality."

"I will go out alone," I said.

"Is that possible?"

I opened the chest of jewels, selecting anklets and bangles. "I will create my own rhythm. None shall die with me today."

The servant bowed and left.

Mother is dancing for the queens again. I like to watch but Aapep is bored and won't stop poking me. I let him drag me away, up to the top of the palace, higher even than the king's patio, to the top of the roof itself.

"See," Aapep says, "our city is the center of the world."

I turn slowly around and see the world is like an immense bowl around us, ringed with distant mountains on all sides. Near the river are the fields and farther from it are the hot sands shining in the noonday sun.

"This isn't the whole world," I say at last.

"Of course it is. There, down the river, are the mountains where my father trades. That is the end of everything."

"No, my mother is from farther away than that, from deep within the sea of grass. And beyond that are more lands still, like the rocky place by a far-off ocean where my father's people dwell."

Aapep thinks about this for a long time, slowly turning around.

"You are right," he says at last. "But there are more lands beyond the mountains in all directions, each way just as far. We are still the center of everything."

"I don't know what's so good about that," I say. "I'd rather see all the other places than be in the center, not moving."

I try to turn the iron bangle on my wrist but it's too tight. Soon they will cut it off and replace it with another, less tight but still too small to slide off. Bangle after bangle until I stop growing and the last bangle stays on forever, like my mother's.

The city does not allow foreigners to live within its walls, unless they are wives of the king or one of the princes. My mother sold her freedom to stay with the man she loved and sold mine along with it. I have always known this, and it always made me feel small inside. The greatest love story in the city, musicians and poets, painters and sculptors were all inspired by my mother's tale. I am included only in a few of stories and none of the art. I am a slave with no great story of sacrifice, only a slave like all the others.

———

It's mid morning when I came out of the palace to perform my dance. The sphinx was above me and I felt her eyes following me as I crossed the sand of the square, stopping in the middle to turn to face her.

Her lion's paws were stained with gore from yesterday and all the days before. The sun was behind her, making her whole body seem to glow with a golden light. I couldn't see her eyes, but that made it easier to face her.

I bowed my head, taking deep breaths. I still didn't know what I'm going to do. My mother came close with her dance of homesickness, but not close enough. Did the sphinx long for some other home, nothing like the sea of grass?

Or did she, like me, long for no home at all?

That thought shook me, it felt so true. I gasped and looked up at her towering over me, certain I was right but still unable to meet her eyes through the glow. Surely she didn't choose to stay here waiting for some puny being to move her to tears? Surely she'd rather fly wherever she chose, hunt and kill whenever hunger struck her. It must be a curse, if the augurs were right. The sphinx was trapped the same as I.

I jingled my anklets, then my bangles. And then I began to dance.

I conveyed failure in all my dance moves. I'm not a girl of the sea of grass, dancing to make the plants grow tall. I'm not a girl of the sand, leaping high and spinning as if the ground beneath me burned my feet, set me sputtering up and up like a drop of water on a hot griddle. I'm too much of the earth for that.

I'm definitely not of fire, the dance most sacred in the city at the center of the world, the dance that showed mastery of the core of civilization itself. I'm not sure I even like cities.

And through it all the only beat was the jingle of my jewelry, that bright sound always marred by the dull ring of my iron bangle.

The last part was harder. I tried to find the dance that was me, that fit my body and soul. Was it a dance of my father's people? Was it something else, something from one of the other ends of the earth? And would I ever know, trapped as I am in the very center?

At last I could dance no more and collapsed to my knees, my body drenched in sweat.

Then I felt a splash on my shoulder blades, a warm rush of water that mingled with my sweat. At first I feared it was blood, it was so very warm, but when I looked up it was to find myself in the shadow of the sphinx's magnificent eagle's wings. She stretched them out, flaring every feather. Then she leaped up into the air and was gone.

In the end I had the king's smiths pound my bangle out to a slightly larger size, one I could slip off and on any time I chose. I was free of it, and yet I didn't want to lose it entirely.

I wondered if the sphinx had gone home, or wandered free, or if she was still cursed, trapped even now in some other city.

If I traveled to enough cities I'd surely know.

"Are you going to find your father's people?" Aapep asked.

"Maybe. Not right away. I think I'll go north first. I'm most curious about the north."

"Will you ever return here?" he asked.

"Surely I must, someday," I said to him. "It's the center of the world."

THE STORY FOR THE LETTERS

imagined my hands were my mother's hands, smoothing and weaving my chaotic hair into a neat braid. Even after days of practice it took several tries and the end result was a mess, too loose here, too tight there, hairs that fell out of the pattern then were woven back in later. There was even a bend in the middle; how had I done that?

"Irrara?" I said. He looked like he was sleeping but usually he wasn't, he just closed his eyes to think.

"I'm not going to braid your hair, you need to learn how to do it yourself," he said without opening his eyes.

"I *did* do it myself," I said. "I wanted you to show me again which one is our mountain."

"It's too hot for that. Just lie still, digest your food."

I said nothing. We had just eaten the last of the black bread, dry and hard even when soaked in water first. It sat like a hard lump in my belly, but there hadn't been very much of it. I preferred not to just lie there with my eyes closed thinking about the food I just ate, or worse the food I wished I had.

So I crept out from under the awning, the bricks of the tower burning my bare feet. I stayed up on my toes and took two giant leaps to the rampart. The sun was starting to move down the western sky; there was just enough shade against the rampart wall for my tiptoes.

"The two big ones flank the river," I said, remembering my brother's words. "We are three over and beyond." I counted three sharply defined mountain peaks, each a sun-baked dusty brown from the long drought. Then I looked between the third and fourth peaks to the blue smudges beyond. Home.

A cloud of dust momentarily obscured my view. I followed it back to its source much closer to the city, on the shores of the trickle of the river.

"They don't think it's too hot," I said. "I bet they have food too."

Irrara was quiet and I thought this time he really had gone to sleep, but curiosity got the better of him and he sat up with a groan to come see what I was looking at.

"They have food, don't they, Irrara? They have caravans bring it to them from their home, don't they?"

Irrara wasn't listening. He shaded his eyes with a hand and gazed and gazed. My brother had the sharpest eyes of anyone I knew. Back home he always found the lost sheep no matter how far across the valley they strayed. When we first came to the tower he would describe the people in the city below and make little stories out of what they were doing. To me it was all a multicolored blur.

"Are they leaving?" I asked hopefully. "Are boats taking them away?"

"They're not leaving," he said then turned and ran down the steps. I tried to run after, afraid to lose sight of him, but I couldn't keep up. I got tired fast these days; what little food I ate just sat in my stomach. It hardly seemed worth the trouble of eating, especially when chewing was so tiring.

Irrara couldn't keep up the pace either, even though the air inside the tower was so sweetly cool after the intense heat on the roof. As we descended the slow spiral stair that wound around the central open atrium of the tower I slowly caught up with him.

There were seven librarians tasked with maintaining all the records of the king, the shelves and shelves of scrolls, clay tablets, and curious objects I was forbidden to touch. For having such an important job they never seemed to be around. As we left the staircase and crossed the atrium only my uncle Illuratum was at his station, his scribe tools on his knees as he carefully copied the inscription from a stone tablet onto papyrus. I knew a few of our letters but he was writing some other language entirely. I sat near him to look at the tablet, mindful not to touch it. My ears had grown double in size since I'd come to the library, I was sure, so many cuffs to the head I'd gotten for just looking like I might touch something.

"They're damming the river," Irrara said and my uncle immediately set his tools aside.

"You're sure?"

"I saw it. I'm sure."

"Come," Illuratum said, struggling to his feet then leading my brother to the door under the staircase.

I had never been allowed past that door. Had my uncle meant for both of us to come? I thought not; in fact I didn't think he even realized I was there. As interesting as the tablet was - and the picture carved on it was interesting indeed, what was that bull-headed man doing to those maidens? - I really wanted to see what was beyond that door.

Plus, the tablet would still be there if I got cuffed and sent back to the atrium.

"Sheshkala," my uncle started to say.

"I'm not touching it," I said, leaning nearer the tablet.

"She'll be fine," Irrara promised. "Sheshkala, I'll be right back."

I nodded, pretending to be engrossed by the tablet. At the last moment I dashed forward, my bare feet silent on the carefully swept stone floor, and caught the door just before it snapped shut, slipping inside quickly in case the lingering light from the atrium drew my uncle's attention.

I didn't like this new place. The bricks under my feet were painfully cold, even damp, something strange indeed in this dry city. It was almost completely dark, only a faint grayness in front of me to lead the way.

I suddenly wished I had my shoes, tight as they were. Back home in the mountains we only had midges to deal with; in the city were more varieties of creepy-crawlies than I had ever dreamt of. In the dark hallway they could be anywhere. They could be *everywhere.*

The thought gave me a shiver of fright, but the word summoned up a memory.

"There are bugs everywhere," my brother had said to me our first night in the tower. "But you know what else is everywhere?"

"No."

"Things that eat bugs."

The idea of bats also lurking around me in the dark was not comforting.

At last I reached the flickering gray light and the tunnel was now a quay, a single rope tied to the mooring post. I leaned over the edge to look down at the boat below. I could see how far up the water usually was, where the stone and brick were worn smooth. I could also see a hand's span of damp wall that was above the still water.

"It's working already," Irrara's voice carried back to me. "They'll be under the gates soon."

I scampered after, not wanting to be so close they'd notice me, but not wanting to be alone in the dark again either. Luckily I was quiet. I was always quiet.

The quay became a tunnel again, darker than before. It followed the same slow spiral as the staircase in the tower above like a mirror-image tower, upside-down, stabbing down into the earth.

My heart was beating faster, as if I were running although in the darkness I walked slowly indeed. I could feel it even in my ears, pressing so hard with each pulse I wanted to cry but I couldn't draw a deep enough breath. I stopped walking, pressing my hands over my ears. It didn't help. Something was inside my skull, squirming around. Only the fear of being alone in the dark got my feet moving again.

At last the tunnel ended in a room as large as the library atrium above. Irrara and my uncle were already on the floor below, but I stopped at the mouth of the tunnel, looking down on the mirror atrium. Braziers filled with blazing coals were set at regular intervals around the circular room, but they did little to dispel the damp cold and seemed to make the shadowy corners all the darker.

"You brought the apprentice down here?" someone asked.

And suddenly I knew why I seldom saw the librarians in the actual library. One by one my eyes found them in the shadowy corners of the room.

"They are damming the river. Soon they will enter the water gates and the city shall be lost," Illuratum said.

"The king will send out every man he has to stop this," said the man I recognized as the head librarian.

"Even if the handful of half-starved men he has left could destroy their dam they'll surely lose their lives in the trying," my uncle said. "We knew this day was coming, the city is lost."

"The Old One knows it too," another librarian said. "His glee is in my head. Oh, I could vomit."

"He grows the stronger as we grow the weaker. We should have destroyed it when we had the chance," the head librarian said.

"We were never strong enough for that."

"We could have tried…"

"The blessed vessel was destroyed; he cannot be moved," said the older of the two women librarians.

"That was always too risky," my uncle said. "He would have been exposed too long."

"He needs to be contained beneath a library," said the head librarian. "We all have heard the tales of this marauder. He delights in destroying libraries. The great library in Pakot was burned to the ground, the river diverted to wash away the remains. Then he salted the earth, as if that could stop knowledge from growing."

"Another dark age is upon us," the woman said.

"There are still libraries to the south in cities with stronger kings," said one of the men.

"Perhaps we should walk away now. Leave this thing to be found. Leave it to be unleashed. Any who survive would have a deep respect for libraries then," the younger woman said.

"I find no humor in your jest," the head librarian said.

"I fear the Old One speaks through you, my friend," Illuratum said to the woman. "Once freed he would feast on the blood of all, not just on our enemies. There would be no survivors."

I sat down on the stairs, careful to stay in the shadow. I had been around enough adults debating each other to know this was nowhere close to resolved.

"Hello."

I was startled by the voice so near, although it had spoken too softly to be heard by those below. It was a boy I'd never seen before, maybe a year older than me.

"Who are you?" I asked.

"I think I should ask that first. I'm always here; you're the intruder."

"You live in the library too?" I asked.

"Under."

"Under the library?"

"Under the city."

"Oh." I looked down at my hands in my lap. I was suddenly afraid anything I said would be the wrong thing, but the silence grew intolerable. "I'm Sheshkala. I come from the north, from the mountain herders, but that's my uncle down there, and my brother is his apprentice."

"Sheshkala is a good name," the boy said.

"Is it?" I didn't know what made a name a good name.

"Aren't you going to ask for mine again?"

"No."

"Then you know who I am?"

"You're not a boy, that's a trick. I've heard all the stories about you, but you've never had a name." I looked down at the librarians still arguing below. "They talk about you as if you were evil."

"Aren't I?"

"I don't think that's the right word. I don't think you're *safe*. I didn't like you when you pressed on my mind before, that was nasty. I suppose I shouldn't even be talking to you. I guess I don't know the proper word for you. Perhaps that's why you don't have a name."

The boy nodded slowly as if I had said something interesting. "You could try 'chaos'."

"I think if you had a name it would be very dangerous to say it out loud, so I shall call you nothing." I knew many stories. I didn't know my letters like my brother, but I remembered any story I had ever been told, and I had always demanded many stories.

"As you like."

I tried not talking to him, I was sure that was the wiser thing, but wise girls don't sneak away from their parents to follow their brother to the low land cities. That was what curious girls did.

"The stories say you fought Tammuk for fourteen days and fourteen nights, and after he at last defeated you he built his palace from your skull, and the city walls from your bones." Then I had another thought. "I think the library is just as old, but no one ever tells what that was built from."

"I believe you know that what's true in stories isn't true in the world," he said.

"I believe in stories."

The boys shrugged.

"If Tammuk built the city out of your bones, then what's left to be you?"

"Silly girl, everything. My bones will be smashed soon, ground to powder and to sand, and I shall be free."

"Then what will you do?"

The boy just grinned, a horrible grin. I turned away and when I looked back he was gone.

One of the women below was speaking, her voice thick with unshed tears of grief and of anger. "If I'm going to die either way, I'd rather take that whole army down with me. They have smashed city after city, they are worse than what we hold contained here. They should know the price of their arrogance!"

Illuratum stepped up to the librarian, holding her by the shoulders and staring into her eyes until she began to weep.

"Forgive me," she said.

"Nothing to forgive," my uncle said. "You have spent more time in this hole than any of us."

"Are we going to flee?" Irrara asked.

"We librarians must stay," the head librarian said. "We have sworn an oath; we go down with the library."

"Then I must too," my brother said.

"No, apprentice, yours is a different task." The head librarian crossed the room to a low reading table and took up a book, bound between sheets of metal that locked in place with a clasp as he shut it then held it out to my brother.

"You must take this to another library, a library in a powerful city far from these heathen marauders, a city as far to the south as you can go, past the sea and further on still. Put it only into the hands of a head librarian; he will know what to do."

"But what about you?" Irrara asked.

"We must seal the Old One and hide him," Illuratum said. "Not forever, none of us has that power, but our souls can strengthen the seal, and when we collapse the tower this room will be hidden. The world will be safe for a millennium."

"Then?"

"The book tells the rest. You *must* get it to a library."

"I will," my brother promised. "Sheshkala?"

For a moment I thought he was calling to me to come with him, but that's not what he meant at all. He didn't even realize I was there.

"The servants will see to her," Illuratum promised. "We have to get to work now, time is short and the spell is long."

Irrara started up the stairs and I scuttled back into the shadows to stay out of sight as he passed, but instead found myself running back to the little boat.

I had followed my brother to the city because I knew all of the stories of the valley already. Irrara had been chosen as an apprentice librarian because he could read and write, but I knew that while he focused on the shapes of the letters he never noticed the story he was immersed in.

The story he carried in the book in his arms was huge, far too big for him to handle on his own. If it had been him on the stairs just moments before, he would have asked that thing that was not a boy its name, and he would have been lost.

He needed me.

But as I had known before, it was important not to be discovered until you were too far away to be sent back.

I hopped in then climbed behind the sacks of supplies waiting in the back. I was just out of sight before Irrara jumped into the boat, clutching the book in one hand and using the other to unmoor us then push away from the wall with a paddle. The water appeared still on the surface but there was enough of a current to carry us down the tunnel.

I could see the normal water level etched into the tunnel wall, and the current one so far below. Surely the water gates were exposed. I strained my ears for sounds of soldiers but heard nothing but the gurgles of the water.

Then the gurgles became a roar.

My brother cried out, trying to keep the boat steady with the one oar. I all but stood up in the back of the boat, looking past him to the gate at the end of the tunnel before us.

For a moment it looked like we would just make it. Irrara ducked low into the keel of the boat to get under the approaching gate. Then another surge of water picked us up too high, dashing us into the bars of the gate.

"Irrara!" I screamed as the boat broke into splinters. I couldn't swim, and the water was churning and full of debris from the boat. Then a hand caught the back of my collar and pulled my up into the air.

"Slide between the bars," he said. "You're small enough to do it."

I turned myself sideways and pushed through. It was narrow and was so tight at my ribcage that it hurt but I made it through.

Clinging to the bar, I turned against the current to look at my brother and saw the boats behind him.

"Soldiers!" I cried. "Quick, get through!"

"I can't," he said, sliding the book between the bars. "I'll try to swim under, but you can't wait for me. And you can't try to go home. They came from behind us, remember? Home is already gone. I'm sorry, Sheshkala. It's just you now. But I believe in you. No one as sneaky as you would ever be caught, not by barbarians like these. Now get the book to safety, go!"

He peeled my fingers off the bar and pushed me back through the water. The current took me. The last thing I saw was his head going underwater just as the boat full of soldiers bumped up against the gate. I heard shouts, the ringing of metal, but the river carried me out into the sunlight and I was too blinded to see.

I floated backwards, looking for my brother, but the waves around me were taller than my head and I could see little but sky.

I reached a point in the river where the current turned lazily around itself and realized I was in a sort of pool. I put my feet down and they touched bottom. The current still wanted to drag me along but I wrapped both arms around the book and put my head down and took step after step until I was out of the water, up the muddy bank, then onward until I topped a little hill. Only there did I collapse on the grass to catch my breath. I was hungry. I had an endless journey ahead of me and no supplies, no money, no energy to see it through.

Surely I could just hide the book, bury it deep and never tell a soul?

A sudden crash of brick and stone had me sitting me back up. I saw the walls collapsing, the library tower crumbling down. The sand was like the city itself crying out in agony.

I think I also heard the voices of the librarians in it, the voice of my uncle. I don't think I just imagined it. The words of power couldn't be obscured even by the roaring destruction of the entire city.

Finally I stood up, giving one last long look at the river, but still no sign of my brother. I would follow it south for as long as I was able, but all too soon I'd have to leave it too behind. Then I would be truly all alone in the world.

I remembered that strange boy's grin and how it had hurt to look at it. Then I hugged the book tight and started walking.

IN THE WASTE PLACES

Ku-Aya sensed the hyenas slinking all around her and her little herd of goats, although they were careful to stay out of sight. Hunger was rousing them earlier every evening, making them bolder. She changed her staff to her left hand to hold her sling ready in her right. Three more hills until they reached home. Too far. She whistled and little Ur-Tur nipped at the slowest goats, goading the herd into a faster trot.

Then a flash caught the corner of Ku-Aya's eye, the last of the sun glinting on metal. Someone, a man in armor, was walking along the river bank. Where was he going at this hour? The sun was nearly down.

"Hey!" Ku-Aya shouted, but the sound ended in a yelp of alarm as the hyenas saw her momentary distraction and lunged out of the shadows. Ur-Tur hurried the goats along as Urda emerged from the herd and faced off with the advancing hyenas, growling menacingly, his corded fur making him look even larger than he already was. The hyenas hesitated but then pressed on, closing in as Urda's growl morphed into a snarl. A fourth tried to slink past but a single stone from Ku-Aya's sling laid him out.

Ku-Aya whistled for Ur-Tur to hurry the herd home as she scrambled to higher ground, sending stone after stone into the moving shadows of the hyenas. Their yelps gave her a bitter satisfaction. She had lost too many goats to their hunger already.

Then Urda cried out in pain and Ku-Aya's heart clenched. She could not see him. She leapt down onto the path and ran downhill to where he had stopped to make his stand. The rocky ground skittered under her sandals, trying to slip her up, and the deepening shadows hid many dried-out roots and jutting rocks.

She just caught sight of Urda, retreating with one flank bleeding badly, the leg not taking any weight, but snarling still as six hyenas slowly crept up to finish him.

Then Ku-Aya was flying through the air, vaguely aware of the sharp pain where her toes had caught a rock before she landed and kept sliding downhill on her belly. She rolled sidewise then around to get her feet under her. She had lost her staff but her sling was still in her hand. Her fingers stumbled to fit a stone into the pouch.

Then there was another cry, not from Urda. This was a war cry, shrill but powerful. The man from the river was standing between Urda and the hyenas, a sword in each hand and a hyena already dead at his feet. He swung his longer blade, and the hyenas pulled back just out of reach. He looked up at Ku-Aya as she spun her sling and Ku-Aya saw an oozing gash across his cheek, narrowly missing his eye. No hyena had done that. Then Ku-Aya saw one of the hyenas make a lunge at Urda behind the man's back and she let her stone fly, whistling past the man's raised sword to take the other hyena on the ear.

He took a step back, closer to Urda, swinging his sword low and wide then looked uphill to Ku-Aya again. His eyes widened in terror and Ku-Aya knew that the one thing worse than hyenas was coming down the hill behind her. Best not to look.

"By the goddess!" the man said, His voice was strangely soft, almost womanly.

"My sling is more use than your blade," Ku-Aya said as she sent another hyena yelping away. "Can you carry my dog?"

The man blinked away his terror with admirable speed and sheathing his swords took the whimpering Urda into his arms. Ku-Aya slung more stones into the pack, but although each found its mark the beasts refused to disperse.

"They don't fear it?" the man asked between labored breaths. The hill was steep, and Urda weighed as much as a goat and a half.

"Not that I've ever seen," Ku-Aya said. "We should hurry."

She led the way, turning often to send more stones into the shadows behind them. She kept her focus close, not looking uphill, but it was hard to ignore the waves of green fog rolling in, the tendrils of smoky green reaching ahead, too close.

They crested the last hill and Ku-Aya broke into a run. Ur-Tur saw her and started barking, urging her on as if she were one of his stray goats, although he was too well-trained to leave his charges while they were still outside their enclosure. She heard the man panting behind her. Then he cried out in alarm.

"It's reaching past me!" His voice was high, ragged with terror.

"Get past the stone!" Ku-Aya said, sliding to a halt when she was inside the ring of standing stones. The man kept running but the grasping fingers of fog behind him washed up against the ring like waves against an invisible dike.

"There's no wall?" the man asked as he looked around.

"Just the stones, city-dweller," Ku-Aya said with a manic grin. "I have to get the goats penned. Bring Urda to my grandfather in the house. Try not to startle him; he's mostly blind and we haven't had a visitor in ages."

The man nodded and trudged toward the light from the hearth spilling across the rocky yard before the open door. Ku-Aya had never seen a city, but she had heard stories. Walls higher than any tower, filled with the bones of the city-dwellers' ancestors. Powerful magic that kept the mountain fog well away from the people within the walls.

This stranger was in for a long night.

The goats needed little encouragement to get inside the pen, bedding down in the little lean-to she had made for them up against the side of the house. Then, carefully not raising her eyes, keeping the green mist out of her field of vision, Ku-Aya walked swiftly to the door of the house, Ur-Tur trotting beside her. It sounded like a breeze was sweeping over the hillside, but nothing stirred her sweaty hair.

She stopped at the door and took the little knife from its ledge over the door. She quickly nicked the heel of her hand, not too deep, not too near the other still-healing cuts, and wiped a smear of blood down the center of the door.

"Quickly," Ku-Aya said, holding out her hand. The man put his hand in hers, barely wincing as she cut his palm. She left him to smear the door, going to her grandfather's side.

"Grandfather, we have to close the door," she said, helping him to his feet and leading him to the door. She cut his palm as lightly as she could and guided his hand to the door. Then she shut the door and dropped the bar, for all the good that would do.

"It's not even moonrise," the man said, absently sucking at the cut on his own palm, far slighter a wound than the one still oozing on his face.

"Soon I think it won't even wait for sunset," Ku-Aya said, helping her grandfather back to his chair. "The rest of our village moved down-river two years ago. The villages around here on both sides of the river are all empty now. Where were you going?"

"Ku-Aya," her grandfather said, sounding as he so often did like he had not yet come out of a deep nap. "What woman have you brought here?"

"Woman?" Ku-Aya repeated, puzzled.

"Oh, I'd forgotten," the man said. He reached behind his neck to untie a leather cord. A smoothed but unshaped piece of lapis lazuli hung from it like a pendant, the sheen of it in the firelight caught Ku-Aya's eyes for a moment. When she looked again to the stranger's face she saw a woman. A tall woman in armor, with swords and arms strong enough to carry Urda over those hills, but a woman all the same.

"That's a nice trick," Ku-Aya said. "I cut off all my hair and started wearing boy clothes when I first had to tend the goats alone. Do they sell such jewels in the city?"

"It was a gift, one of a kind," she said, holding it tight in her fist then tucking it away in a pouch on her belt.

"I am Mezem. This is my granddaughter Ku-Aya." Ku-Aya's smile was less one of welcome to their guest than happy surprise. Her grandfather sounded fully aware, a rare thing.

"Enanatuma, of the House… but no, not anymore."

A whistling gust spun around the house, building to a shriek like a dying woman's last curse, then faded away.

"The mist is past the stones," Ku-Aya said.

"Until this morning I had never been outside the walls of Ummur. Now I can never return." Ku-Aya could see the woman was fighting back tears and deliberately turned away, kneeling beside Urda where Enanatuma had laid him near the hearth.

"Come closer to the fire," Ku-Aya said over her shoulder. "I'll dress that wound for you."

Urda whimpered at the sound of her voice and she bent down to kiss his nose.

"How's your dog?" Enanatuma asked.

"He'll be fine. Only one really bad bite that will keep him off his feet for a while but he'll recover."

What was she going to do? She couldn't take the herd out without him.

Ku-Aya was relieved to find the woman stoic once more as she sat on the little stool by the fire. Ku-Aya gently cleansed the gash, being particularly careful where it came so close to her eye.

"This is from a blade," Ku-Aya said.

"A killing blow."

"It doesn't look so bad."

"No, I don't suppose it does. Still, but for that mere scratch I'd be home still with my husband and children."

Ku-Aya didn't know what to say to that. At last she said, "my father died and the next day all the other villagers left. It's just me and grandfather now. The whole world changed in just one night. Father was inside the stones, in the safe place. One of the goats was still out there and he was trying to call it back. I remember the bleating; it was lost in the fog but not scared, not hurt.

"Then the fog rolled past the stone and took my father. Nothing was left in the morning but his bones. I didn't see it happen but grandfather did. It's why he's blind now. I stayed with him but all the other villagers left that very day. We thought the stones would always protect us."

"You said this fog comes earlier now? And it's getting stronger?" Enanatuma asked.

"Yes," Ku-Aya said, folding a clean rag into a thick wad and pressing it over the wound. "When I was young these hills were full of life. Sheep and goats grazing on green grass, people everywhere, boats up and down the river. Now it's nothing but hyenas and barely enough scrub for the few goats we have left. Why did you come this way when you left Ummur?"

The woman said nothing as Ku-Aya tied the bandage to her head as best she could. Then she touched her wound as if assessing Ky-Aya's work.

"I have a friend who was planning to go north, to find the lost city of the goddess. Because of this, this fatal wound that left me living this ghost of a life, she is trapped in the city as I am trapped out of it. I owe it to her to do what she no longer can."

"But all the cities are in the south. Do you know what she's talking about, grandfather?"

He didn't answer, but the voices outside the walls came again, and a sound like hundreds of rats scurrying over the mud brick walls and thatched roof overhead.

"It's like this every night?" Enanatuma asked.

"It's just getting started," Ku-Aya said.

"But if it's broken past your stones someday it will break past your door."

"Not tonight," Mezem said.

Ku-Aya was certain Enanatuma in her armor and swords was used to far finer fare than their soup of too-old goat meat and too-young onions, but she gave no sign of it. By the time they were done eating the roar outside the walls was constant, tittering, laughing, screaming, sobbing all at once. And the skitter of nails on the walls was becoming the rapping of knuckles, ever more insistent.

"You didn't leave with the others because your grandfather was too weak to travel?"

Ku-Aya nodded. "He was lost in fever for days and days and the others would not wait."

"Why do you stay now?" Enanatuma asked.

"My family is here, I cannot leave them," Ku-Aya said.

"Your grandfather can travel now, surely."

"I meant my father, and my mother and baby brother."

"They power the stones," Enanatuma guessed.

"There is a place," Mezem said, so suddenly the other two both jumped. "When I came down out of the mountains to live with my son-in-law's people, my brother did the same. His daughter settled among fisher folk on the shores of the salty lake to the north of here. It is a good-sized town with a wall, not as large as the southern cities but strong enough. I am certain it still stands."

"In the morning I will help you move north," Enanatuma said.

Ku-Aya was about to object when, as if in answer, the mud bricks behind her grandfather cracked like a thunderbolt. Ku-Aya ran to the wall. It was still standing but a long crack split the bricks like jagged lightning from floor to ceiling.

"I can see the fog!" she cried, but quickly turned away. Her grandfather never spoke of what he had seen. The last thing he had ever seen.

"Come closer to the fire," Enanatuma said. "We should rest while we can; we have a long day ahead of us."

But the voices whistled and screamed through the crack, mocking them and their faith in the safety of the hearth. Ku-Aya sat with Urda's head on her knee, Ur-Tur in her arms, and waited for morning.

Her grandfather usually made her wait until she could see sunlight around the door frame but today he let her peek out the crack in the wall and when there was not a hint of green she slowly opened the door. The sun was not quite up. Everything was still and gray.

"Look," Enanatuma said and Ku-Aya followed her pointing finger. Tendrils of green were disappearing over the hilltops like the train of a fringed gown sweeping over the dirt.

Behind them Mezem was moving about the house, packing what little they had of value.

"I won't go," said Ku-Aya.

"Ku-Aya, we already stayed her far too long," her grandfather said. "Life has left this place. We cannot stay for the sake of the dead."

"You're a mountain nomad, you don't understand," Ku-Aya said, angry tears flashing in the corners of her eyes.

"You're half-nomad yourself," he reminded her. "Your mother was nomad."

"But she chose to remain here."

"Just as you must choose to move on," Enanatuma said, putting a hand on the girl's shoulder. "I know how hard it is, but you know I'm right."

Ku-Aya crossed her arms, sniffling angrily but not speaking. Finally she gave a tight nod.

"I will leave the dead behind if I must," she said, "but not the living."

"Your grandfather is coming with us," Enanatuma said, although the quirk of her eyebrow said this time she knew that wasn't who the girl was referring to.

"No, Urda," Ku-Aya said. "And Ur-Tur, and the goats."

Enanatuma frowned. The dog was still lying by the hearth, too injured to rise, Ur-Tur guarding over him. Enanatuma looked at Ku-Aya and the girl pushed her chin just a little higher in the air.

"I know that look," Enanatuma said. "My daughter gives me the exact same look when there's no use arguing with her."

"I'll fetch the cart for Urda," Mezem said as Ku-Aya shouldered the pack he had filled for her and jogged across the yard to release her goats. Enanatuma followed, already wearing her own pack. She knelt beside the protecting stone, touching the faded writing.

"Can you read it?" she asked Ku-Aya.

"I don't read. Can you?"

"Not this, the letters are strange. I think my friend could if she were here."

"My mother, baby brother and father all lay together under that stone. I'm meant to join them, when my time comes." The last of the goats ran out of the pen and she shut the gate.

"I do understand, Ku-Aya," Mezem said, groping until he found and squeezed her arm. "I like it no better than you. I swear we will return for them but today we must leave them behind."

Ku-Aya nodded her acceptance then murmured it, but hot tears ran down her face and her hands clenched into useless fists.

Enanatuma loaded Urda onto the little cart. They had no animal to pull it so she picked up the front end herself and pulled it behind her. Ur-Tur got the goats moving and Ku-Aya took her grandfather's arm to guide him.

They stayed close to the river until mid afternoon when they reached the bend Mezem had told them to watch for, where the river had cut a basin out of the hills to make a pool of slowly turning water. The trail to the top of the basin was too narrow for the cart, so Enanatuma took Urda into her arms once more and lugged the heavy dog up the steep path. Ku-Aya came behind, the empty but still heavy cart balanced on her shoulders. Mezem followed more slowly, feeling his way with a stick, Ur-Tur close on his heels to watch his progress.

At the top of the basin was a long, flat grassy valley. Enanatuma and Ku-Aya laid down their burdens and rested on the cool grass as Ur-Tur left Mezem in their charge and went back for the goats.

"How much further?" Ku-Aya asked, not liking how close the sun already was to the tops of the hills. They were much higher than the hills back home.

"We're in the valley? Do you see a gap between the mountains at the far end? The lake is between those mountains."

Enanatuma and Ku-Aya exchanged a despairing look. They would never get so far before sunset.

Ku-Aya tried to take a turn with the cart but even over the smooth, level ground it was too heavy for her.

"Don't worry, I can keep going," Enanatuma said. "It helps to see our goal."

Ku-Aya would agree, only that goal never drew any closer. They walked for hours but the mountains remained hazy blue shapes at the end of a neverending expanse of green.

"It's a shame we can't stop, the goats could gorge themselves a hundred times over here."

"I think we should stop," Enanatuma said, pointing with her chin. "There."

"What is it?" Mezem asked.

"A house, one house all by itself," Ku-Aya said. "I don't see people."

"It must be abandoned, like your village. It will have to do, we don't want to be caught out in the open after sunset."

The house was not only abandoned, it had only ever been half built. Ur-Tur and Ku-Aya herded the goats inside the walls and Mezem hung their blankets over the window and door, but there was nothing to be done about the lack of roof.

"Do we mark the doorframe with blood?" Enanatuma asked.

"No point," Ku-Aya said. "That was a gesture of bonding with my ancestors buried under the stones. No one ever died here. Or I guess I mean were buried. I knew we should have brought my family's bones with us. It's not safe without them."

"We have no protection at all?" Enanatuma asked.

"Perhaps some," Mezem said. "My people were tent dwellers. We couldn't carry our dead with us, but there is magic in hearth and home. Light a fire and we'll share some food, make this shell of a building into a proper home for at least one night."

The sun was long gone behind the hills, the first stars winking out of the darkening blue above them when Ku-Aya handed hot pan bread to the other two, Enanatuma shared out a simple soup she had made from the last of the onions, and Mezem divided the last hard lump of goat cheese.

"Don't look up," he said suddenly and Ku-Aya fought the urge to see what he had sensed. It had to be the fog rolling over them. "Keep eating. We should talk too, like a family."

"You grew up in the mountains?" Enanatuma asked when Ku-Aya had failed to find anything to say.

"When I was young the mountains were full of nomads, moving the sheep from pasture to pasture," he said. "But we became fewer each year. My daughter and niece were fine young women, beautiful and skilled, yet could find no suitors. My brother and I had to come down to the lowlands to find them husbands. We returned to our beloved peaks but life became impossible there."

"Why?" Ku-Aya asked. "When I was little you said you missed my mother but I don't think that was the reason you came to live with us."

"Perhaps we had displeased our goddess, but our young would not thrive, not our own children or the young of our flocks."

"Did the fog come?" Enanatuma asked in a whisper. Or it may only have seemed a whisper; the voices in the fog around them were growing louder.

"No. Not while my brother and I were still there."

"It sweeps in from higher ground."

"I know nothing about it," grandfather said. "I'm not sure this is the right sort of conversation."

"What did you see?" Ku-Aya demanded over the roar around the walls. "Did something in the fog kill my father? Or was it the fog itself?"

"I don't know!" Mezem cried. "What burned my eyes burned my mind. Sometimes I can almost remember. Then I scream. Scream!" He ended in a screech that was quickly joined by the screeching of the goats around them.

"Don't look!" Enanatuma shouted, pulling the blanket from the doorframe and flinging it over their heads. Ku-Aya reached behind her, snatching the blanket from the window. She and Enanatuma held the two together overheard, the ends tucked tight beneath them. Mezem settled himself on another corner, Urda and Ur-Tur together holding down the last.

The space under the blankets was hot and close, and the goats screamed in agony around them.

"Can't we save them?" Ku-Aya sobbed. "They came so far."

The others didn't answer; there was nothing to be said. Enanatuma took her hand and squeezed it tight.

"Do you have more magic? Other stones with other powers?"

"No," Enanatuma said. "If it comes to it, I have my blades."

Ku-Aya cried out in near hysterical fear. "Something is touching me! Through the blanket, it's poking, pinching…"

Enanatuma drew her shorter blade but Mezem caught her hand.

"The blanket is all we have."

"We left them behind! We shouldn't have left them behind. Now I'm all alone without them. I don't want to die so far from them. How will they find me?"

"Ku-Aya, you must calm yourself," Enanatuma said sternly. "If this is our end we should meet it with dignity. Think of what you have loved best in this world. Remember your family. Hold those thoughts close to you and don't let the monsters in. Don't listen to their voices." She broke off with a hitch, but if there were tears in her eyes it was too dark for the others to see.

Then Ku-Aya began to sing. Enanatuma did not recognize the language but the tune was familiar. Mezem added his voice to his granddaughter's, reaching out to clasp her hand as he did. Enanatuma removed her hand from the hilt of her blade and took his other hand, still clasping Ku-Aya's with the other. The two dogs snuggled together inside their circle. Enanatuma listened to the song go around a few times then chimed in when bits she could make out repeated again. Each cycle she added a few syllables more, fixed pronunciation mistakes, caught nuances, until finally she could sing the whole song through.

And it was morning.

They let the blankets drop and rose on stiff legs. All around them were the skeletons of goats, their bones intermixed and picked quite clean.

"What was that?" Enanatuma asked. "That song."

"It was something my mother used to sing to me when I was little when I had nightmares," Ku-Aya said.

"It's a mountain song," Mezem said. "We all sing it to ask for the goddess's blessings and protection. I don't even understand most of the words, it's a very old song."

"I'm glad I've learned it," Enanatuma said. "It fills a hole in my heart I didn't even know was there."

Urda was limping around the house, nosing at the remains of his goat pack with a sad whine. Ur-Tur was running around outside, anxious to continue their journey.

"The answer to all this is in the mountains," Enanatuma said, looking past the village to the dark gray peaks beyond.

"Now that we know how to survive in the open, we can travel there without fear," Mezem said, leaning on his staff.

"We? You mean to come with me?"

"If you'll have me, for what use a blind guide would be," he said. "I have a longing to feel myself in my home one last time, to smell the air and feel it's cold bite on my cheeks."

"Ku-Aya?" Enanatuma gently asked. The girl was standing with her back to them but not in anger; she was watching Ur-Tur bounding back to them, six dirty gray shapes lumbering through the grass ahead of his driving barks. Sheep.

"These live while my goats were taken?" she said.

"Perhaps like the hyenas they are untouched," Mezem said.

"I think the fog only attacks humans, and things in the care of humans," Enanatuma said. "This meadow is full of rabbits, great fat ones."

"They've been on their own for a while, that's certain," Ku-Aya said, touching each sheep one by one, looking at their teeth and faces. They were lean but unharmed. "Look at the state of their fleece. They haven't been sheared in years."

"Ku-Aya, are you coming with us?" Mezem asked. "You can see where your mother was born, where she lived until she was older than you are now."

"I've missed her every day since she died, she and my baby brother who never even got a name," Ku-Aya said, focused on working a nettle out of one sheep's fleece. "And I know you miss your daughter that you had to leave behind in the city, Enanatuma. A part of me wants to stay with you both. But it doesn't feel like the right choice for me, and I think I'm old enough to make my own choices."

"Of course you are," Enanatuma said. "I confess I was hoping we'd be friends."

"Maybe someday. But for now Ur-Tur just brought me a herd. I rather feel responsible for it."

"I know you will take good care of them," Mezem said, hugging her tightly. "You handled our goats all alone for so long. I am sorry, I imagine you felt like I abandoned you too, and now that I'm well again, or at least better, I'm leaving."

"I understand," Ku-Aya said. "But there are people in that village. I look forward to living with people all around me again. It's going to be like magic."

"We will return when it is done," Enanatuma said. She didn't add "if we are able" but Ku-Aya heard it all the same.

"Your aunt is Shiptu, she will look out for you," Mezem said. He hugged his granddaughter tight. "She will know you; you look just like your mother."

"As if my mother ever cropped her hair."

"She will know you."

Then Enanatuma put his hand on her arm and they walked away.

Ku-Aya turned back to her dogs. It would be a slow walk with Urda's limp, but the day was long and the journey short. Ur-Tur hied off, sensing more sheep lost in the tall grass. Ku-Aya spun her sling in her hand absently, eyes alert for danger.

She looked like her mother, but in her heart she was a low-lander, a herder like her father. The walls of the village called to her. Perhaps they too could take comfort in what she had learned about the fog.

SCI-FI SERIAL PODCAST!

Check out my new monthly podcast of serialized science fiction: THE TALES OF THE CHAI MAKHANI TRIO!

Elyot loathes the massive Commonwealth ships that hover menacingly over his home world of Adghal. He hates the Commonwealth enforcers who harass the populace even more. But with his mother missing and presumed dead, Elyot keeps his head down and strives to avoid notice. And he succeeds until the day two strangers enter his life...

New episodes of this sci-fi serial drop every 1st of the month.

Now streaming on Apple Podcasts, Google Podcasts, Spotify, Stitcher and more. Also available in eBook and print everywhere books or sold. For a complete episode listing, check out the page on my website.

COMPLETE SERIES: THE TRAVELS OF SCOUT SHANNON

The complete six-book series THE TRAVELS OF SCOUT SHANNON begin with book one, Under Falling Skies.

Scout Shannon's whole family died the day the Space Farers dropped an asteroid on their domed city. Now she lives alone, out in the wild with only her dogs for company. She prefers it that way.

But Scout finds herself at a crossroads. One road leads back to a quiet life snug under the protective dome of a city. The other road leads to a life in the rebellion, a life of adventure and excitement but also danger. Dare she try to find the rebels hiding in the hills?

Then a chance encounter with a stranger from the other side of the galaxy threatens to derail what remains of Scout's life. The entire galaxy awaits her, if she survives the next four days.

"Under Falling Skies", a young adult science fiction novel, set on a remote planet with a distinctly Old West feel. For fans of gunslinging women and young girl assassins. And dogs.

Under Falling Skies, the first book in THE TRAVELS OF SCOUT SHANNON, available everywhere now.

NEW SERIES: THE RITCHIE AND FITZ SCI-FI MURDER MYSTERIES

The Ritchie and Fitz Sci-Fi Murder Mysteries starts with Murder on the Intergalactic Railway.

For Murdina Ritchie, acceptance at the Oymyakon Foreign Service Academy means one last chance at her dream of becoming a diplomat for the Union of Free Worlds. For Shackleton Fitz IV, it represents his last chance not to fail out of military service entirely.

Strange that fate should throw them together now, among the last group of students admitted after the start of the semester. They had once shared the strongest of friendships. But that all ended a long time ago.

But when an insufferable but politically important woman turns up murdered, the two agree to put their differences aside and work together to solve the case.

Because the murderer might strike again. But more importantly, solving a murder would just have to impress the dour colonel who clearly thinks neither of them belong at his academy.

Murder on the Intergalactic Railway, the first book in the Ritchie and Fitz Sci-Fi Murder Mysteries.

ALSO FROM RATATOSKR PRESS

Also from Ratatoskr Press, The Witches Three Cozy Mystery Series by Cate Martin, a mix of mystery and magic that begins with Book 1: Charm School.

Amanda Clarke thinks of herself as perfectly ordinary in every way. Just a small-town girl who serves breakfast all day in a little diner nestled next to the highway, nothing but dairy farms for miles around. She fits in there.

But then an old woman she never met dies, and Amanda was named in her will. Now Amanda packs a bag and heads to the big city, to Miss Zenobia Weekes' Charm School for Exceptional Young Ladies. And it's not in just any neighborhood. No, she finds herself on Summit Avenue in St. Paul, a street lined with gorgeous old houses, the former homes of lumber barons, railroad millionaires, even the writer F. Scott Fitzgerald. Why, Amanda can practically hear the jazz music still playing across the decades.

Scratch that. The music really, literally, still plays in the backyard of the charm school. Because the house stretches across time itself. Without a witch to protect this tear in the fabric of the world, anything can spill over. Like music.

Or like murder.

The complete series is out now, and it all starts with Charm School.

FREE EBOOK!

Like exclusive, free content?

To get two prequel short stories to THE RITCHIE AND FITZ SCI-FI MURDER MYSTERIES as well as a bonus prequel novelette to the completed six-book series THE TRAVELS OF SCOUT SHANNON, signup for my monthly newsletter at KateMacLeodWrites.com.

Thank you!

ABOUT THE AUTHOR

Photograph © 2016 Jonathan Conklin

Kate MacLeod has written stories which have appeared in Analog, Strange Horizons and Mythic Delirium, among other places. She is also the author of two young adult science fictions series: The Travels of Scout Shannon, and The Ritchie and Fitz Sci-Fi Murder Mysteries. She also contributes to a serialized science fiction podcast called The Tales of the Chai Makhani Trio. She currently lives in Minneapolis, Minnesota.

Find out more about the author and sign up for her newsletter at KateMacLeodWrites.com.

ALSO BY KATE MACLEOD

Novels

The Slums of the Solar System:

Mitwa

The Mars of Malcontents

The Whole World for Each

Books 1-3 Box Set

The Travels of Scout Shannon:

Under Falling Skies

In Quaking Hills

Among Treacherous Stars

Against Impassable Barriers

Over Freezing Altitudes

At Galactic Central

The Travels of Scout Shannon Books 1-3

The Travels of Scout Shannon Books 4-6

The Travels of Scout Shannon Books 1-6

The Ritchie and Fitz Sci-Fi Murder Mysteries:

Murder on the Intergalactic Railway

Murder in the Skies

Body in the Catacombs

Death on the Summit

An Undiplomatic Murder

A Lethal Betrayal

Sci-Fi Novellas

The Intergenerational Tree

I Rise into a Daybreak

Caper Novellas

The Third Pole Job

The Twelve Days of Christmas Job

10-Story Collections

Tales of Blood and Ink

Tales of Old Gods and New

5-Story Collections

Tales from Heian-Kyo and Others

Tales from the Edges and Ends

Tales from Forgotten Days

Tales from Ancient and Future Times

www.ingramcontent.com/pod-product-compliance
Lightning Source LLC
Chambersburg PA
CBHW032012180726
48283CB00008B/2637